Pulling t

## ALSO BY K. J. PARKER

*The Long Game*
*Inside Man*
*The Big Score*
*Prosper's Demon*
*My Beautiful Life*
*The Father of Lies* (collection)
*Mightier Than the Sword*
*The Devil You Know*
*Downfall of the Gods*
*The Last Witness*
*Blue and Gold*
*Purple and Black*
*The Two of Swords*
*Savages*
*Academic Exercises* (collection)
*Sharps*
*The Hammer*
*The Folding Knife*
*The Company*

*Snow White and the Seven Samurai*
*Valhalla*
*The Portable Door*
*You Don't Have to Be Evil to Work Here, But It Helps*
*The Better Mousetrap*
*Blonde Bombshell*
*The Outsorcerer's Apprentice*
*The Good, the Bad and the Smug*

# PULLING THE WINGS OFF ANGELS

K. J. PARKER

A TOM DOHERTY ASSOCIATES BOOK

NEW YORK

PULLING THE WINGS OFF ANGELS

Cover art by Micah Ulrich
Cover design by Christine Foltzer

A Tordotcom Book
Published by Tom Doherty Associates
120 Broadway
New York, NY 10271

www.tor.com

Tor® is a registered trademark of Macmillan Publishing Group, LLC.

ISBN 978-1-250-83577-2 (ebook)
ISBN 978-1-250-83576-5 (trade paperback)

First Edition: 2022

*He's just another bully, when he pushes folks around*
*He's a bigger, badder bully; I don't want him in my town*

**—Leslie Fish**

# Pulling the Wings Off Angels

"First," said Florio the gangster, "I'm going to cut off your nose and make you eat it. Then I'm going to cut off your ears and make you eat them. Then I'm going to gouge out your eyes and make you eat them. Then I'm going to cut off your balls, fry them in a bit of your own fat, and make you eat them. Unless—"

"Yes?"

Florio is about forty, fair-haired, stocky, just under medium height. If he says something, he means it; that's his gimmick, in a world where everybody's got to have one to stand out from the crowd. Florio keeps his promises, like God. Personally, though, I think the reason for Florio's outstanding success in his profession is his imagination, which is vivid, lurid, and just quirky enough to make you piss yourself, as I'd just done.

"Unless," Florio said, with a smile, "you do a job for me."

"Consider it done," I said quickly. "Really. I mean it."

His goons had nailed me to a door. Other gangsters

tie people up. Florio has big dome-headed roofing nails hammered through the web of your palms, taking care to miss the major veins. The religious imagery is quite deliberate; under that rough exterior, Florio is a devout templegoer, well versed in the scriptures.

"That's the ticket," Florio said, and nodded to one of the goons, who passed him a claw hammer. It's the only way to get a nail out of a door, but it means they had to use my wrist as a fulcrum. I think I may have screamed, but Florio and his people were very kind and pretended not to notice.

(In case you're wondering, I owed Florio a quarter of a million staurata. That's an awful lot of money; enough to pay for a warship, or keep a regiment in the field for three months, or build a large temple; the annual tax revenue of the entire Mesoge is eighty thousand staurata. Moral: Never play cards with notorious underground figures. If you do, and you get dealt a hand with four aces, fold immediately.)

"Get some bandages and a basin of warm water," Florio said, "and some of that plantain extract. There's bound to be a scar," he told me, "but in your line of work that's probably no bad thing. What's the technical term? Stigmata?"

I managed a feeble grin. Actually, believe it or not,

some of my fellow seminary students pay money to have the same thing done, albeit in a rather more humane fashion. Anything to get an edge in the cutthroat world of ecclesiastical preferment.

"Thanks," I said.

"All part of the service." Florio nodded to his pet doctor, who started fussing about with swabs and tweezers. He always has a qualified medic around on these occasions, to tell the goons where the nerves and arteries are, with the proper medical names for them. That's class, if you ask me. "Now then, this job you're going to do."

I'd reached the point where the dead chill was starting to thaw into pain and nausea, so my voice wobbled a bit. "Fire away," I said.

"I want you," Florio said, "to get me an angel."

Oh for crying out loud.

~

This nonsense about my family. It's got to stop.

There are two versions of it; the one everybody seems to know, and the truth. If I tell you both, you can choose between them. Piece of cake.

There's absolutely nothing to say about my family on my father's side until you go right back to the original

Maenomai met'Auzen. He was one of the fifty companions who followed Scaevola to Issecuivo, crossing the vast ocean to look for a country nobody really believed in. After Scaevola found and conquered the New World, Maenomai was given a province to govern. As luck would have it (they drew lots) it wasn't one of the really valuable ones. It had gold mines, but they were mostly worked out, and Maenomai spent what little he was able to grind out of them trying to improve the agriculture on his new estates and plantations, because all the peasants were poor as rats, and prosperous tenants can afford to pay higher rents than starving ones. That didn't work very well; he tried to introduce Old World crops and livestock, and of course they shrivelled away and died in the blistering heat, so he had to let the natives go back to doing what they'd always done. He ruled his share of the empire for twenty years, ending up with rather less than he'd started with when he and the others crowded round an old hat to see who'd get what; then he sold the lot to his surviving partners and went home. He was still fabulously rich, by Western standards, and everyone agreed it wasn't bad going for the fourth son of a minor country squire. His descendants gradually reverted to type, whittling down Maenomai's inconceivable wealth by means of bad luck and bad management until they were once again obscure provincial gentry; at which point, my father married my mother, for her money.

Which brings us to my grandfather, on my mother's side. Everything is, of course, always about him. He died before I was born so the following is all hearsay, rumour, and legend. For example, there are no surviving records to verify his claim that he was born in prison, or that his mother got pregnant by one of the warders to save her neck from the noose. Fair enough. Paper costs money and so does clerks' time; people like that don't tend to get written about. If that part of the story is true, he grew up in the slate quarries—son of a serial offender, three guesses how he was going to turn out, no point letting him go since he'd only find his way back into custody sooner or later.

According to family legend he had a blissfully happy childhood—the only kid in the camp, spoiled and cossetted by five hundred convicts and a hundred guards, entirely unaware that his surroundings were in any way unusual. His mother was dead by the time he was ten, but it hardly seemed to matter to a boy with six hundred devoted aunts and uncles. He went to work on the slate as soon as he was old enough to push a cart—the guards made him a little toy one out of scraps of packing cases—and since nobody ever got round to telling him that quarrying slate isn't supposed to be fun, he spent all day doing what he loved best, without boring aunts and uncles or stupid lessons getting in the way. Everybody saved a few bits and pieces from their rations for the poor orphan boy and he worked from sunrise to sunset, pushing carts and then swinging a pick, so by the time he was fourteen he was enormous; nearly six feet tall and still growing, broad as an ox and strong as a bear. At which point, one of the guards took it into his head to teach the kid how to box.

He turned out to be good; so good that the guards pooled their savings, bought him a free pardon from the provincial governor (awkward, since he'd done nothing to pardon, but I imagine they found a way round that) and sold him on indentures to one of the leading trainers in Auxentia City.

The indentures were for ten years, but the trainer let him off after eight. He was a good boxer, but not quite good enough; he stopped a stiff left to the side of the head in a routine exhibition match at a country fair somewhere, and that was the end of him as a professional fighter.

The punch left him blind in one eye and generally flaky, but he was still fit, agile, and enormously strong, so he gravitated from fighting to general showman stuff, tumbling and trapezes and the high wire, until his balance went, and he had a bad fall, after which he quit performing and moved over to the management side. Everybody in the troupe liked him, and he turned out to be very good at business. He realised that what audiences wanted was a bit of sophistication with their spectacle; little stories to frame the action, like they had in the arenas in the big cities. He started making up little plays. They went down well, so he hired a couple of proper writers, and before long he'd turned the tumblers into a touring theatrical company, specialising in nautical melodrama, which was just starting to get big at that time. At the age of thirty-one he moved to Choris Seautou and took the lease of a large but rundown theatre on the unfashionable side of the river. He called it the Palace of Joy, soon shortened to the Palace; and now you know precisely who I'm talking about and what happened next.

His big break came when he hit on the idea of doing a deal with the City Prefect (who just happened to be seeing a lot of one of his leading ladies at the time) whereby convicted criminals were executed onstage at the Palace as part of the play, rather than on a gibbet in the prison yard where nobody could see. He got his house authors to rework all the classics to include execution scenes, sorted out some foolproof security protocols to make sure none of the criminals could escape or make an embarrassing fuss, and announced a series of special gala matinees; advance booking only, with a range of ticket prices to suit all pockets, from two staurata for a box to twelve trachy for standing room in the pit, nine trachy for the upper gallery. After a slightly tentative start he was soon playing to capacity houses, and the only problem was getting enough talent to satisfy the demand. Soon he was shipping in convicted criminals from all over the province, and his friends in government circles added forty-six new crimes to the schedule of capital offences, just to maintain the supply. He was also smart enough to get out of that line of business well before the reaction set in, so that when the do-gooders had onstage executions banned and all his rivals lost substantial sums of money, he'd already moved on to burlesque, comic extravaganza, and light opera, which proved to be the next big thing.

That required him to become respectable, but that wasn't a problem. He built the Gallery of Illustration on a prime site right in the centre of Choris, and before long it was the hottest ticket in town. He'd always been moderate in his tastes and inclined to a quiet, frugal lifestyle, and he got his writers to work up appropriate small talk for him to use whenever he met people of quality. Pretty soon he didn't need any of that. Everyone says he was one of Nature's gentlemen, the proverbial diamond in the rough. Natural good manners, a pleasant, open disposition and a net worth estimated at two million staurata made him welcome in the highest circles of society, and at age forty-two he married his second wife, my grandmother, poor as a rat but first cousin to an earl. They were, by all accounts, ideally suited and devoted to each other, and he never looked at another woman until the day he died.

In short, the fairy-tale rags-to-riches success story, and every trachy he ever made was earned fair and square without hurting anyone or grinding the faces of the poor. All he did was give people what they wanted, with the useful knack of knowing what they wanted before they knew they wanted it. Some nitpickers said nasty things about the public executions, but the majority of right-thinking people held that Justice must not only be done but be seen to be done, and two thousand paying customers seeing it done every night, with musical accompaniment and fireworks to follow—what could be more edifying than that?

Born scum, died a gentleman, and wherever he went

and whoever he was introduced to, everybody was always pleased to know him, even dukes and princes. It only goes to show that you can make it in our society provided you've truly got what it takes. In which case, there can't be much wrong with the way things are, now can there?

Anyhow, that's where the money came from, and at least some of it is still there, despite my father's best efforts to get rid of it. He sold the theatres and the various other sidelines, because gentlemen don't do trade, and he bought land; huge estates in Chaerea and the Mesoge, just before some fool made peace with Blemmya and the market got flooded with cheap Blemmyan corn. But that was all right, because land is land, they aren't making any more of it, and if it doesn't produce enough income to pay the bills you can always mortgage it. To pay off the mortgages he married my mother, which cost him twelve thousand acres and a copper mine by way of dowry, but worth it because a fleet of grain freighters came with her, just right for the grain run to Blemmya, except that shortly after that some fool started the Second Blemmyan War and that was the end of the overseas grain trade; so my father swapped the freighters for vineyards in Mavalis and a munitions factory with government contracts, which paid handsomely until some fool ended the war and everyone was suddenly wallowing in cheap, high-quality Blemmyan claret. My father and my mother didn't see eye to eye a lot of the time. I think they mostly argued about business.

None of which really matters; except perhaps to explain why I felt the need to make a lot of money when I should have been cramming for my theology finals, and why I thought I had the sort of luck it takes to pull off a big score, and probably why it didn't work out. It also introduces the theme of inheritance, which you're going to hear an awful lot about as we go on. Don't say I didn't warn you.

Anyway, that's the true story. I expect you know the other version, so I won't bother with it.

~

"It's all bullshit," I said. "It's just a myth. There never was any angel."

Florio looked very sad. "Pity," he said. "I like you, even though you cheat at cards. But if you're right then there's no force on Earth that can save you. Have you ever tried nose? They say it tastes a bit like chicken."

One of his goons handed him a knife. "I'll get the

money," I screamed. "I promise."

"A quarter of a million?" He smiled at me. "I don't think so. If you'd had any way of raising large sums of money, you'd never have tried to cheat me in the first place. You must have been really desperate to try that."

No, not really. I thought I could get away with it. "My father," I said. "He'll pay."

He shook his head. "He hasn't got a quarter of a million. Well, strictly speaking he has, but he'd need to sell a lot of land and nobody's buying it since the war, so by the time he's paid off the mortgages he'd be getting pennies on the stauraton, and that's assuming he can find a buyer. That's the trouble with old money, you think you're loaded and then when pitch comes to shove you find out you're as poor as dogshit. It's a real shame your father sold the theatres. I'd have taken the Palace and the Gallery like a shot. I've always fancied being in show business."

I'd been examining the knife. It was really close to my face, so I had a splendid opportunity to see how very sharp it was; a coarse stone followed by a fine one, then honed on the rim of a glass. The point, no pun intended, about a knife is that the work it does is irreversible. Once a bit's cut off, you can't stick or stitch it back. I don't know about you, but personally I think irreversible things should be avoided at any cost. It's a matter of principle.

Which led me on to the question of faith. I didn't believe in the angel, but Florio presumably did; like I said, he's very devout. His faith could buy me time, and time changes things. Without faith, I'd run out of time, the greatest irreversible of them all. Faith, of course, is just another way of saying opinion. In my opinion there aren't any angels because there's no God; but a lot of people, the majority in fact, believe in the Invincible Sun and all His heavenly hosts, angels and ministers of grace and all the rest of it. Who's to say my opinion's worth more than theirs, just because it happens to be true? That would be unspeakably arrogant.

"Fine," I said. "You win."

Florio laughed and nodded; the knife disappeared as though it had never existed. "Of course I do," he said. "I always win at everything. Hadn't you noticed?"

~

Always: a hardworking word, never out of fashion. I was always intended for the Church from the moment I was born. If I'd been a girl, I'd have been married into Trade, for money, but I was a boy, so that meant God. A bit like my grandfather, really; he was a criminal from the moment the umbilical cord was cut, because of heredity. By the same token, third sons of the met'Auzen are destined for the priesthood, and we generally end up as abbots of minor houses or bishops of the less prestigious dioceses. It means God provides for us, thereby reducing the load on the family finances, and we pray for the family souls, so that angle is covered.

I believed in the Invincible Sun when I was a kid. After all, there He was, up in the sky, so bright He hurt your eyes. It was only when I went to the seminary and started studying to become a priest that I stopped. There's nothing quite like the scriptures for killing faith stone dead. Actually reading them and thinking about what they said evaporated my belief like spit on a hot stove. I can't say I was sorry. Up till then, my life had been constrained and restricted by all sorts of rules, most of them arbitrary and quite unreasonable; thou shalt not steal, for crying out loud, thou shalt not commit adultery, where's the fun in that? Once they'd dissipated into the mist, I realised I could do what I liked. Provided I managed to keep out of jail, there was nothing to stop me having a whale of a time. I rather liked the sound of that.

Meanwhile I carried on with my studies. In fact, I

began to apply myself to them as never before. Being a priest means all sorts of good things; tenure for life, exemption from secular courts and laws, not to mention being forbidden to marry, which means you can share your bed with whomever you like instead of having some lumpen heiress inflicted on you by your family. In order to enjoy yourself properly, of course, you need money. Being a priest would see to that in due course, but in the meantime, I had to make do with temporal resources, namely a less than generous allowance from my father.

I don't consider myself a sensualist by any stretch of the imagination, so I'd probably have been just fine if I hadn't met Zosima; but I did, and that was that. Heavenly bliss. But she costs per hour more than a skilled stonemason makes in a year, including overtime and the usual kickback on materials, and the trouble with paradise is, it's addictive. The more of it you get, the more you want. Then want becomes need, and you're screwed.

Hence my pressing need for money, lots of it in a hurry. That in turn led me to card-play. It transpired that I was really rather good at it, which surprised me. I'd never been more than barely competent at anything in my entire life, but for some reason I could beat people at cards and take money off them, so I did. What Florio thought was cheating, by the way, was no such thing. It was pure skill and a certain amount of luck, which ran out spectacularly quickly when it most mattered. My luck put four aces into my hand, just when Florio said, let's make this interesting, how about I raise you a hundred thousand?

Consider luck: is it just a mealy-mouthed way of saying God? My own words betray the fact that I apparently believe in luck, at some visceral level. Luck would have to be some external agency powerful enough to control what happens; in which case, it meets the basic criteria for being God. In other regards, of course, it has little to do with the form that God conventionally takes. It doesn't seem to worry about whether or not you've been good; nor does it give a damn if you pray to it. It's there for a while, and then it goes away again. I think of it as the way everything in the house shakes when one of those heavy carts loaded with slate goes by on the way up from the quarries. The cart has its own agenda, which has nothing at all to do with me, but it makes my house shake, which affects me, so understandably and misguidedly I take it personally. My guess is, whether or not I win at cards depends on some sort of cart going past on some sort of road, but it's not *about* me. It's just stuff happening.

~

I'd promised Florio an angel. Fine. What Florio wants, Florio gets.

The last reported sighting of the angel was in the chapel of my grandfather's house at Dis Exapaton, so that's where we went. My grandfather built the chapel first and then the rest of the house—weird behaviour unless you happen to believe in the untrue version of the family history, in which case it makes perfect sense—and it stands on its own in a remote corner of the deer park, out of sight and mind of the big house, where my aunt Domna lives on the rare occasions she isn't in Choris. Nobody about, in other words. There wouldn't be anyone to see us and my screams wouldn't carry as far as the lodge or the gardeners' cottages. Swell.

Family legend has it that my grandfather got quotes from all the leading artists of the day for doing the chapel walls and ceilings in fresco, then paid one of the scene-painters from the Gallery a twentieth of the lowest quote; in return he got truly exquisite artwork and the scene-painter was able to retire and buy a vineyard.

That part of the story might just possibly be true. The vestibule ceiling looks like the Ascension as depicted by a talented artist used to doing transformation scenes for pantomimes; it has that sense of innocent wonder that you grow out of when you're eleven, and I think it's lovely. It's not trying to be Great Art, and so that's exactly what it succeeds in being.

It helps that the model for Divine Grace blowing the trumpet in the dead centre of the composition was the most beautiful actress of the day, my grandfather's first wife. She made her name as the best principal boy of her generation, then discovered she had the voice of an angel and turned to light opera; everything male with a pulse in Choris was in love with her, and then she married my grandfather. Anyway, she's still there, gorgeous in heavenly pink as the eye of a storm of joy and hope on the chapel ceiling; these days seen only by gardeners, it's true, when they come and go to collect the tools they store in the vestibule, but nonetheless a thing of beauty and a joy forever.

I mention her because, as far as I was concerned, she was the only angel who ever resided there, but naturally I wasn't going to tell Florio that. My take on the family legend, for what it's worth, is that she really was the angel, allegorically speaking. There was this wonderful creature—beautiful, talented, bursting with life and joy, bright and fresh as a spring day—and my grandfather married her to keep her from signing a contract with a rival impresario. They lived together for five years, during which time he completely crushed her spirit; then she got sick and died, and my grandfather married again, purely for status, resulting in (among other things) me. That's what really happened, and the version of the story you know is just a metaphor: a bad man kidnaps an angel and breaks her wings so she can't fly away. The bit about keeping her locked up in a dark cellar presumably refers to her quitting the stage and coming to live at Dis Exapaton, where I imagine she was bored out of her mind.

Anyway, there she was, and Florio, all due credit to him, craned his neck to gaze at her for about twenty seconds, which is a long time to be uncomfortable. "I like that," he said. "Question is, could you get it down from there without smashing it all to hell? You'd have to cut out the whole ceiling and haul it away on a winch, but would it hold together or just crumble away?"

"It doesn't belong to me," I said. "And my aunt doesn't like me very much."

He lowered his head back to a more natural angle. "And who can blame her?" he said. "Fuck it. Who needs pictures if you can have the real thing?"

Awkward. He was in for a massive disappointment, and so far I'd frittered away the time I'd bought so dearly with nothing to show for it, apart from a black eye and a split lip I'd acquired when I mistakenly imagined the goons weren't watching me. If only I'd had a bit more time and a certain degree of unaccompanied movement. I could've hired some out-of-work actress and dressed her up in shiny rags and a pair of stage wings, and maybe just possibly Florio would've bought it long enough for me to think of something. As it was, here we all were in the centre of the vestibule floor, next to the steel ring by means of which you pull up the marble trapdoor that leads to the cellar, which of course would prove to be empty. I remember thinking: dear God, I really and truly wish You existed, because then You could send a real angel, and I wouldn't have to get cut up and fed to myself—Not that I don't deserve it, but that's surely beside the point. You don't turn to God for justice; that's what judges and lawyers are for. You go to God for mercy, or you would if He existed, which He doesn't.

Florio nodded to a goon, who tried to pull up the trapdoor and failed. So three of the four goons got a belt and passed it through the ring and heaved, while the fourth goon put his arm round my neck, with the crook of his elbow under my chin, to keep me from being silly and getting myself hurt. The goons heaved and the belt broke and they went sprawling on the ground; the hell with it, Florio said, stop fart-arsing about and fetch a couple of sledgehammers. Then he turned to me. "Doesn't look like anybody's been this way in a while," he said.

"Not since my grandfather's time, I don't suppose," I said, with difficulty. You try saying *I don't suppose* with someone's arm crushing your windpipe.

"That's grand," Florio said. "It means nobody's been here before us and stolen the angel. I was worried about that."

Well, it opened up a possible avenue of justification which I hadn't previously considered. There's no angel in the cellar because some hooligan must've broken in and stolen her; no, I couldn't see it working, any more than *a dog ate my homework.* Wouldn't do any good even if he believed it. The main difference between those two all-powerful entities, Florio and God, is that Florio is under no obligation to be fair.

There were sledgehammers in the pile of gardeners' tools, and the goons didn't take long smashing the trapdoor into gravel. "Anybody remember to bring a lamp?"

Florio asked. No, but there were lamps in the tool stash, filled with oil, wicks trimmed. Someone got one lit, and we were good to go. Oh well, I thought. It's been a horrible life, but it'll soon be over.

The lamp showed us a stepladder. Florio nodded to a goon. "Lead the way," he said. The goon didn't look happy, but he nodded and vanished down the ladder into the hole. Florio handed him the lamp. "What can you see?" he said.

"You're not going to believe this," said the goon.

~

My grandfather, so the untrue version says, kidnapped an angel. How would you go about that, exactly?

I speak as a qualified theologian, and I really don't know. But if it was me, and if I believed, I'd set out to achieve an epiphany; not because it would be easy, but because I can't think of any other way.

An epiphany, for crying out loud. Serious holy men spend their entire lives trying to achieve one, fasting and praying day and night for years, decades, a lifetime. An epiphany, so they taught me in second year, is a visitation by Divine Grace in material form. It's not a vision, something you think you see which isn't actually there.

An epiphany is *real*; you can reach out and touch it, you can stick your fingers into the wounds and bring them out sticky with the blood that was shed to save us. (And what would that get you? Blood on your hands. Been there, done that, as you'll eventually see.)

Something like that, it goes without saying, doesn't just call for single-minded devotion, which is just a polite way of saying effort. You need faith; faith so monumental that it can make the impossible happen. There's an old story, which I've always liked, about a holy man who yearns for an epiphany. So he leaves the city and his rich family, sells everything he owns and gives the money to the poor, and builds a hermitage in the wilderness. For sixty years he lives there on his own, praying and fasting. He's taken a cartload of books with him—the complete scriptures and all the commentaries—but as the years go by, he stops reading them, because he knows them all by heart. He stops praying too, because he's said it all so many times that he can't see the point anymore; either the Invincible Sun has heard him or He hasn't, and isn't there a commandment somewhere about Thou shalt not nag the Lord thy God? So he spends most of his time outside in his garden, growing food for himself and the very occasional passerby. He grows cabbages and leeks and turnips and peas and nine different varieties of beans, onions and shallots and carrots, strawberries, raspberries, redcurrants, grapes, cherries, apples, pears, plums, marrows and squashes and pumpkins the size of an ox, though he doesn't like pumpkin very much, and who can blame him? And one day, God comes by and leans over the gate and stands there for a while, watching the old hermit raking over a seedbed. The hermit notices him and says hello, and they have a nice chat about greenfly and pumpkin blight and what to do about carrot-fly, concerning which the Omniscient turns out to be pretty well-informed, although the hermit's able to teach Him a thing or two about earthing up fennel. Then He says he has to be getting along and they part; nice chap, the hermit thinks to himself, and not a bit like how you'd expect. And then he dies, but he doesn't go to heaven because he's already there.

Nice story, but that would be completely useless for the present purpose, because what I needed to get Florio off my back was an angel, not God; the monkey, not the organ-grinder. If God showed up, He'd just give me a sad look and say, Told you so.

~

"Get out of the way," Florio said, "I'm coming down."

He disappeared down the ladder, leaving me with the three remaining goons. Understandably enough, they were a bit concerned. Their master, to whom they were ferociously loyal, had just gone down a ladder into a dark cellar in response to a cryptic remark, in a building they knew for a fact to be quite ridiculously haunted. There was a distinct possibility that something bad might happen to him down there, and they were worried. Meanwhile, leaning up against an exquisitely painted wall along with the rest of the gardening tools was a muck fork.

I haven't had much experience of violence, thank God, but I've always reckoned that your average garden shed contains weapons of such awesome ferocity that you don't need to bother with armourers. Take, for example, the traditional four-pronged muck fork. Which I did and stuck it into the nearest goon before he had a chance to stop me. Then, for the good of my health, I stuck the other two. They hadn't been expecting anything like that from a gutless coward like me, and on any other day in human history they'd have been quite right. For the record, I'd never killed anyone before, or even drawn blood that wasn't my own. I think they were as surprised as I was when they died.

"What's going on up there?" I heard Florio yell, down below in the cellar. Nuts, I thought. The perfect resolution to the story would've been me slamming the trapdoor back in place, sealing Florio and his goon in a richly deserved living tomb; but the trapdoor was just so much rubble, so I couldn't do that. I had a significant tactical advantage; I was armed with an extremely effective weapon, and they'd have to engage me singly, with one hand on the ladder. Or I could do the sensible thing and run like hell. Yes, I thought, let's do that—

Florio put his head up above the edge of the trap. I guess he must have seen the dead bodies, and me with the fork in my hand, its tines glistening. If so, he dismissed them as trivial. "You really want to come and see this," he said. "It's amazing."

"Fuck you," I yelled, and lunged at him with the fork. The ease with which he took it away from me, single-handed and with no apparent effort, put my heroic achievement in killing the other three into appropriate perspective; beginner's luck, obviously. He threw the fork away. This wasn't a time when forks mattered. "I want you to see this," he said. "You're a priest. You know about this stuff."

"Fuck you," I repeated, though it wasn't really germane to the issue.

"Come and look at this and we'll forget about the money."

"Really?"

He gave me a look: forty per cent contempt, the rest bewildered joy. "This changes everything," he said. "Come on."

I wasn't sure I wanted everything changed. "What's going on down there?"

"Come *on*."

On the one hand, I'd just killed three bad guys with a garden fork. On the other hand, a bad guy had just taken the fork away from me as if from a small child. I decided there wasn't a viable military solution to my difficulties, so diplomacy it'd have to be. Or I could run like hell. People had run away from Florio before. Some of them got a relatively long way, measured in yards rather than inches. Screw it, I thought. Have you no intellectual curiosity at all?

He scrambled up the ladder and stood aside to let me climb down it. I found myself in a cellar, your basic underground room with cobwebs. I could see the cobwebs because it was very well lit in there. Something crunched under my foot. I glanced down and saw the smashed shards of the lamp Florio had taken down with him.

Oh, I thought. The light wasn't coming from any lamp.

"That's her, isn't it?" Florio said, coming up behind me. "Your angel."

Even assuming he meant *your* to be second person plural, as in the Met' Auzen angel, it was a degree of proprietorship I didn't want to acknowledge at that point. "I don't know, do I?" I hissed. "I never saw that woman before in my life."

She looked at me. Because she was such a highly efficient light source, I couldn't really see her all that well; I got an impression of shining translucent white skin and golden hair, and that was about it. "That's not a *woman*," Florio hissed at me. "That's an angel. Are you blind or something?"

I had to say something. "If she's an angel, where's her wings?"

"Don't you *see*?" Florio was more excited than angry: impatient, I guess you could call it, because I was being so slow and stupid. "This changes everything. If there's an angel, there must be a God. If there's a God—"

Quite, I thought. It does rather change things. Then I thought: hang on . . .

"That's not an angel," I said. "I have no idea what it is, but it's not an angel. It can't be."

"Have you gone crazy?" Florio said. "Look at her, for crying out loud. It's obvious."

"No," I said, taking a step back. "Think about it. Whatever it is, it's a prisoner here. Has been for I don't know how long." I waited for the penny to drop, but it just hovered, like a hummingbird. "You can't lock up angels," I said.

I think I was going a bit too fast for Florio. "Can't you?"

"Of course not, you idiot. Angels are manifestations of God. God is omniscient and omnipresent, so inevitably He would know if a bit of Him was being kept locked up in a cellar. And He'd do something about it, don't you think? So that's not an angel. I don't know what it is, but I'm guessing it was put down here for a very good reason. I think we should leave now."

"No," she said. "You're wrong."

That voice—voice of an angel; you hear them say it all the time, whenever there's a new girl in town. So-and-so is the best actress since Andronica and she has the voice of an angel. It wasn't really like that, though; my grandfather would never have married someone who sounded like that, because there'd have been no danger of her getting lured away by a rival management. Mostly it sounded hurt.

"Go on," Florio said.

"This room," she said. "He had it built specially. Someone taught him how to do it, a professor from the seminary. Saloninus. You may have heard of him."

That made no sense. Saloninus was my tutor in patristics and moral philosophy. Or someone with the same name. He's no spring chicken, but he wasn't nearly old enough to have been around in my grandfather's day. "What does it do?" Florio asked.

"In here, He can't hear us. Or see us. He can't come in here at all."

"Bullshit." The word escaped from me like a chicken getting loose from the run. "Sorry, but it is. He's everywhere, at all times. He knows everything."

She shook her presumably beautiful head. "Not in here," she said. "That's why Saloninus is the most brilliant genius who ever lived. He designed this room. He made it possible for a human to escape from God."

Florio and I looked at each other. Now please take note of that. Under normal circumstances, our relationship was strictly that of predator and prey: You'd be more likely to see the eagle sharing a glance of fellow-feeling with the sparrow, or the lion offering to buy the lamb a drink. In the face of what we'd been suddenly forced to confront, however, Florio and I were just two human beings teetering on the edge of Understanding. "Did you know about this?" he asked me.

"Fuck, no. I never heard about any magic room. I don't believe any of this shit." I stopped. "I didn't believe," I amended. "I thought it was all just allegory for the failure of my grandfather's first marriage. I don't believe in God. Didn't believe." My legs were too thin and spindly to bear the enormous weight of my head. I sat down, without first arranging for anything to sit on, and landed uncomfortably on the floor. I tried to get up, and found I'd got my knee on something soft. A man's back. The other goon.

"He's fine," Florio said. "He passed out when he saw . . ." He shrugged. "I know how he felt," he said. "It's a lot to take in all at once."

Just out of interest I checked the goon's pulse. What pulse? Maybe he'd left it in his other jacket. A weak heart, presumably; well, that just left Florio and me. Not that it could possibly matter. Everything had changed.

Florio could see that, too. The more he thought, the less expression on his face. He looked like he'd just died in his sleep. "Just to clarify," he said.

The angel looked at him. "Yes?"

"There's a God. The Invincible Sun."

"Yes."

"And you're an angel. Part of Him."

"Yes."

"And in here—" He hesitated. "You can't tell lies, can you?"

"No, of course not."

"In here," Florio said, "He can't see or hear anything. It's like He doesn't exist."

"In this room," she said. "Yes."

Florio breathed in deeply, then out again slowly, two or three times. I've seen fighters in the arena do that, just before the start of a bout. Apparently it's supposed to centre you or something like that. "One more thing," he said. "You've been here how long?"

"Eighty-six years."

"That's a long time. Why didn't you simply leave?"

She looked at him. Then she stood up and turned round. On her back, round about the shoulder blades, were two wings. Not quite, there used to be wings there, but at some point they'd been snapped off, and now new ones were slowly growing back.

"Ah," said Florio. "I see. How long before—?"

"Another five years," she said. "Then nothing on Earth can hold me, not even this room."

"Got you. But until then—?"

She turned back again and faced him. "Weak," she

said. "Approximately the same strength as a mortal four-year-old. That seems to be how it works, anyway. The fact is, I simply don't know. There's never been anything like this room before. There's nothing about it in the field manual."

"Excuse me." I elbowed my way past Florio, who didn't seem to mind; he was still thinking, so hard it practically made the walls shake. "I just wanted to ask you something, if that's all right."

She smiled at me. Smile of an angel. "Shoot," she said.

"It's about forgiveness."

"Ah," she said. "That."

I wasn't sure I liked the sound of that, but not to worry. "They teach us in first year that it's never too late to repent. Is that right?"

"It's true. I'm not so sure that it's right. Sorry, it's not my place to moralise. Yes, it's true."

I noticed that she was glowing steadily brighter. I think it was because we were talking to her. "So if I repent now, I can still be forgiven."

"Yes and no."

Not the sort of answer you want in those circumstances. "Excuse me?"

"Yes, as a general rule. No, not in here, because He can't hear you. You'd need to go back up the ladder."

Angels are traditionally supposed to give rise to a wide range of emotions, from exhilarated joy to black despair. I never heard about irritation being one of them, but there you go. "If I do that," I said, "and I sincerely repent—"

"You'll be fine," she said.

"Of course he'll be fine," Florio interrupted. "He hasn't done anything."

She gave him a sour look. It changed her face entirely. "Don't take any notice of him," she said. "He doesn't know what he's talking about."

"Bullshit," Florio said. "He got dragged here against his will, and he hasn't done anything wrong. Killing the lads doesn't count because that was self-defence."

She turned her head and smiled at me. "They were his nephews," she said.

I looked at him. "Yeah, well," he said. "My sister's boys, I promised her I'd look after them. But that doesn't matter now, everything's changed. And he hasn't done a damn thing you can have him for. Well? Isn't that true?"

"Absolutely not," she said. "He's guilty of greed, covetousness, failure to alleviate the sufferings of the poor, six counts of not turning the other cheek—"

"Oh come on," Florio said scornfully. "That's nothing,

everybody does that. What I mean is, he hasn't done anything bad concerning *you*. This whole business. Well? Has he?"

She sighed. "I never said he had."

"No, but you implied it." Florio was grinning. "While we're on the subject."

"What subject?"

"Forgiveness," he said. "Repentance. It's true, isn't it? You can do any damn thing you like, and provided you repent afterwards, you're fine. In the clear. Well? Answer me."

"Sincere repentance," she said sulkily. "Which I don't think you're capable of."

"Really?" Florio laughed. "Shows how much you know. You bet I can be sincere."

"Really."

"Oh yes." He was still grinning, but it was that hard grin, the one he has in common with wolves. "Because it's all about knowing, isn't it? If you don't know, it's different. You think there may be a God but then again there may not, so on balance maybe what you did was bad and you're going to get in real trouble because of it, but you don't *know*. And then you get to thinking, if I say I'm sorry and give all this money back to the people I took it from, and then there's no God after all, how dumb is that? And then you say to yourself, so maybe there is a God, but maybe all this repentance stuff is bullshit, and I'm going to burn in hellfire anyhow for what I've done, so why not keep the stuff and enjoy it while I can? That's called doubt, isn't it?" he asked me, as resident theologian. I nodded. "Doubt," he repeated. "But I'm not doubting anymore, because I *know*. So I'd have to be dumb as dogshit not to repent and feel really, really bad, *knowing* that if I don't I'm bound to fry. Isn't that right? You tell me."

She had a sort of baffled look. "That's not repentance," she said. "That's just fear."

"Same thing." He looked really pleased with himself. "Well, isn't it? What's the only reason anybody ever obeys any law? Because they're scared of what'll happen to them if they don't, and they get caught. That's all your virtue is, it's being scared out of your wits. And you know I'm right, because if it's not like that, then why do you have all that hellfire and eternal damnation? It's a punishment. A deterrent. Meaning, do as you're told or we'll make you wish you'd never been born. That's all your virtue is." He paused to widen his grin, something I wouldn't have thought possible if I hadn't seen it with my own eyes. "Okay," he said, "you win. I'm scared. Really, truly scared. I know I'm going to get caught. That's fine. Therefore my repentance, when it comes, will be fucking sincere. Until then—" He beamed; the smile, I have to admit, of an angel "—Until then I can have some fun. And you're my ticket."

"But it's not sincere," I said. "We both know that. You've more or less admitted—"

"In here, yes. Where He doesn't know what we're saying."

Before I could move or do anything, he lunged past me, grabbed her hair in one hand and one of the half-grown-back wings in another, and gave a short, sharp yank. The wing came away in his hand; the bone, even the ball-shaped socket at the end. She screamed. Did you ever hear an angel scream? Once you've heard it, nothing is ever the same again.

"That hurt," he said.

"Yes." She was barely audible.

"You can hurt, in this room. You can feel pain."

"Yes."

"It's true, then." He looked like he'd just bought an old coat in the market, and the pockets turned out to be stuffed with gold coins. "He knows about this room? Come on, answer me."

"Yes," she whimpered. "He knows it exists, but not where or when."

"And He knows you're missing."

"Of course. I'm part of Him. You'd know if someone cut your nose off, wouldn't you?"

Which struck a chord with me, for some reason. "What the hell have you done?" I said.

He still had the wing in his hand. Silver liquid, like mercury, was dropping off it and pooling on his dead cousin's face. "Nothing," he said, with a smirk. "Nothing anybody can prove, anyway. And you know what they say. No witnesses, it never happened. As far as He knows, I haven't done shit."

"Yes, but—"

He turned to face me. I'm actually about an inch taller than he is, but you'd never know it. "No witnesses," he said. "I just pulled the wing off an angel, and I could go out there right now and He wouldn't know a thing about it."

He was between me and the ladder. I don't suppose that was pure chance. "Just a second, for crying out loud," I said. "So you can beat up on an angel and get away with it. So what? What good would that do?"

He nodded. I'd asked the right question; well done. "None whatsoever. That's why He's got to know."

I considered him, from a moral and theological point of view. Crazy as a jaybird. "That's fine," I said.

"I'm leaving now. I'll get your money for you as soon as I can, I promise."

His hand was on my neck before I saw it move. I could feel his thumb in the hollow between my collarbones. He'd need to press in about three-quarters of an inch, and that would do it nicely. "Yes," he said, "you can leave. In a moment, when I've told you what I want you to do."

~

Ten minutes later I was outside, out in the fresh air, feeling the warm sun on the back of my neck. This, I thought, would be a very good point at which to run away. Except—

I looked round, getting my bearings. From where I was standing I could just make out the green dome of the big house, built by my grandfather to please my grandmother. The dome is copper; in his day it would have been polished and shiny, scooping up the Sun's rays and flinging them back in His face, but dome-polishing costs money, so these days it's green. My aunt Domna lives there now. She married Genseric Rutilian shortly after his father's creditors foreclosed on the family estates in the Transbohec;

it was a fire sale rather than a love-match, but they got on reasonably well together for about five years, and then Uncle Genseric considerately died. As his widow, my aunt is entitled to call herself the hereditary Empress of Beal Regard; the empire collapsed about two hundred years ago and I think the Hus live there now, but no matter, the title is entirely valid and it gives my aunt a great deal of pleasure, so what the hell. It means she gets asked to a lot of functions in the City, though she hardly ever goes.

The park is really rather fine. It was laid out by the leading landscaper of the day on the Echmen pattern, so you can imagine what it's like; caves, grottos, waterfalls, camellia and rhododendron thickets, little bridges over geographically impossible streams that feed into perfectly circular lakes. I remember using it as an example in a theology tutorial; if God created the world, why isn't it ordered and beautiful like my aunt's garden, instead of being a random and largely inhospitable mess? I got an extra mark for original thinking, cancelled out by a point deducted for failing to recognise the possibility that His idea of good taste may not be the same as ours.

A substantial failure when you come to think of it. Naturally, all societies create God in their own image.

He's perfect, so He must be like us and not a bit like them across the border. He thinks like us, obviously; He likes what we like and hates what we hate, and here's Scripture (recorded, translated, and edited by us) to prove it. The possibility that He might not see things the way we do never enters into our heads, because we're His people and the sheep of His pasture, made by Him according to His specifications, so clearly the way we are is the way He thinks the ideal human being ought to be, so what we intuitively believe must automatically be right. Simple logic. I defy you to think otherwise. But just suppose you and I are wrong. Just suppose He exists (now proven beyond a shadow of a doubt) but He has very different views from the ones we instinctively credit Him with—

So there I was, walking in the garden, and He came looking for me. "Here I am," I said, and sat down on a rustic bench to make it easier for Him to find me.

He wasn't what I'd been expecting. I'm not sure what that was, but He wasn't it. I'm hopeless at people's ages, especially kids, but I'd put Him at about fifteen; pink-skinned, like a slave; long, red, curly hair, freckles, blue eyes, a savage, a slightly lower form of life. You snap your fingers, and people like that bring you clean towels. "You're not Him," I said. "Surely."

He shrugged. "I am what I am," He said. "Deal with it."

I had an idea we'd got off on the wrong foot. "I'm sorry," I said. "You're challenging my preconceptions, I can see that now. You've chosen to appear in an inferior form so as to teach me a lesson about prejudice and humility."

"Who are you calling inferior, blueskin?" He grinned. "This is me. You've got my angel. I want her back."

Cutting to the chase: a divine attribute, clearly. "Of course," I said. "Unfortunately, she's not mine to give."

"I know." He frowned. "Florio the mobster has her hidden somewhere, I can see it in your thoughts. But where—" The frown became a scowl. "I can't see where. You know, but I don't." Sigh. "That Saloninus is going to be in so much trouble. You too, I hasten to add."

"Me? I didn't do anything."

"You really believe that, how sweet." A thin, pink-skinned kid smiled at me. I was having a really hard time just talking to him without my lip curling, but here I was, talking to God; an epiphany. "You're guilty by association and under the rules of joint enterprise. Not to mention inheritance."

"Excuse me?"

"The sins of the fathers, stupid. To the fourth and

fifth generations. Your grandfather kidnapped my angel. You were born guilty."

I opened my mouth and shut it again, took a deep breath. "I accept that," I said.

"You do? It's completely unfair. But it's the rules."

"Yes," I said. "It is."

"Think who you're talking to. Of course you don't accept it, you're just saying that. But it's fine, because you're going to get me my angel back. Also, I want to know exactly where this horrible room is, so I can bury it under a million billion tons of rock." He winced. "Not being able to see it gives me a headache. It's like an itch you can't reach."

"As I said," I told him, "she's not mine to give. I'm here to pass on a message, that's all."

"Fine," he said, "You'll keep, I'll settle up with you later. What's the message?"

"From Florio," I said. "He wants you to make him king of Chosroene."

Stony dead silence. I think even Florio would've been intimidated by it, and he's the bravest man I ever met. Not that that's saying anything. "Does he, indeed."

"Yes. He wants to be king of Chosroene for the rest of his natural life. Or thirty-five years, whichever is the longer. Then, when he dies, his people will release the

angel from the room and you get her back. That's what
he wanted me to tell you," I said, stressing the pronouns.
"And that's me done, and I'm out of it."

"No you're not. You're not out of anything until I say
you are."

I chose my words carefully. "Surely that would be a
little bit unfair?"

That got me a full noonday stare. "You're your grandfather's grandson," He said. "Is it fair that you were born
to wealth and privilege and you've never had to do an
honest day's work in your life? No. Is it fair that you
should inherit his sins?" Shrug. "It doesn't matter, because the definition of fairness is what I want it to be.
Now then, where's he holding my angel?"

"In a cellar under the chapel, just over there," I said.

He closed His eyes. "I can't see it." He sighed. "It's no
good. You have no idea how frustrating that is."

"I can take you there."

"Pointless," He said. "I could be standing right next
to it and I wouldn't be able to find it. Fine." He breathed
out long and slow. "Go and tell your friend he can be
king of Chosroene for thirty-five years."

Are you kidding, I thought. "Are you sure?" I said.

Not the right thing to say. "Now that's blasphemy,"
He said. "Thou shalt not impute doubt to the Lord thy

God, not if you've got even the remotest inkling of what's good for you. He can have Chosroene and Procyra and Sirupat and the Chaim Peninsula." He grinned. "Which will more or less guarantee him a long and bloody border war with the Sashan, but don't tell him that, I want him to find out the interesting way. In fact, he can have all the kingdoms of the Earth as far as I'm concerned. It's the good old magnification-to-gravity ratio, of which I'm so very fond."

"The magnification—?"

"The bigger they are, the harder they fall." Divine grin; not a pleasant sight. "Go on, then, tell him. And I hope he makes you a provincial governor, at the very least. You deserve to have some fun, while you can, bearing in mind what's inevitably going to happen to you later."

"Excuse me," I said. "What's gravity?"

He looked at me. "Scoot," He said.

∼

"It worked," I told Florio. "You successfully blackmailed God. You're going to be in so much trouble."

Florio grinned. He's a thoroughly horrible man and utterly terrifying, but I can't help admiring his resilience. Things that have me curled up in a ball gibbering just make him stop and think for a moment, and then he carries on. "I don't know about that," he said. "He didn't give you any details, did He?"

"Absolutely not," I said. "Just *he can be king of Chosroene for thirty-five years.*"

"Thirty-*five*? I thought we said thirty."

"Yes, well," I said. "I thought I was going to have to negotiate, so I pitched high."

"No problem, that's great," he said. Behind him the angel sat cross-legged on the stone floor, steel collar round her neck, chained to the wall. She was motionless and her eyes followed every move Florio made. I decided I'd have to get her some straw to lie on. "Thank you."

"And you also get Procyra and Sirupat and the Chaim Peninsula," I said. "And I didn't even ask for them, He just added them in, for good measure."

"Hey," said Florio. "That's not bad. Where the hell is the Chaim Peninsula?"

I'd been wondering that. "Don't ask me," I said, "I'm a theologian, not a cartographer."

"We need a map." He stopped. "No we don't. You," he said, turning and facing the angel. "Tell me where—"

She gave him a sad look. "Northeast of Angkola,

where the Siruister meets the sea. You wouldn't have heard of it," she added, "it hasn't been discovered yet."

"That," Florio said gravely, "would explain it. Ah well, the more the merrier. Sirupat too, eh? Cool. There's gold mines on Sirupat."

I shrugged. "Maybe He likes you."

"That I doubt." Florio sat down on the floor and cupped his chin in his hands. "It's probably a trick, but not to worry. We'll think of something when the time comes. Look, about the actual mechanics of all this—"

"Search me," I said. "I don't suppose He's going to hand it to you on a plate, though. Presumably you've got to go out there and seize the throne or something." I paused for a moment. "Why Chosroene, incidentally?"

"Because it's a fabulously wealthy absolute monarchy with an effete and decadent royal family," he said. "Also, I was born there."

"Ah."

He nodded. "Probably still got family there," he said. "My mother sold me to a slave dealer when I was six, to buy food to see the rest of the family through the winter. Best thing that ever happened to me, actually, leaving there and coming here. If I'd stayed in Chosroene I'd be a starving peasant."

"If you'd stayed in Chosroene," I pointed out, "you

wouldn't now be God's worst enemy. Still, I expect you know what you're doing."

"Damn right I do," Florio said. "But I wish He'd been a bit more specific. Tell you what. Why don't you go back out there and ask Him?"

"I've got a better idea," I said. "Why don't you ask Him?"

He laughed. "Fuck that," he said. "Me go out there and leave you to mind the angel? I don't think so."

I took a deep breath. "We need to talk about that," I said.

"No we don't."

"Yes we *do*." I felt very brave, meaning scared stiff, but I couldn't see that I had a choice. "Don't do all that stupid scowling and pulling faces," I said. "You need me or you'd have killed me already. Besides, He made it pretty clear that I'm in the shit just as much as you are."

"Really?" He raised an eyebrow. "But you haven't done anything."

The angel made a faint throat-clearing noise. "Told you," she said.

"You shut your face. You haven't done anything," he repeated to me. "And don't let Him tell you otherwise. Still, it doesn't matter what you have and haven't done. It's what you're going to do that's important."

"Exactly," I said. "And we need to talk about it."

He grinned. "Cool," he said. "All right, here's what you're going to do. You're going to stick with me, and I'll make you governor of Buciris province. Well? How about it?"

Buciris: where even the poorest of the poor eat off gold plates and wipe their arses with silk. "I don't want that."

"Seriously?" He shrugged. "Fine. What do you want?"

"Not to burn in hell for ever and ever."

"Don't worry about that," Florio said casually. "It's not going to happen. Oh come *on*," he added, as I made some sort of unhappy noise. "You think I'd get into all this without a plan? Of course I've got a plan. I'm not stupid."

A plan. So that was all right. "Are you out of your tiny, tiny mind?" I said. "You can't have *plans* when you're fighting Him, it doesn't work like that."

"In here it does," he said quietly. "That's the joy of it. You know, remind me to get hold of this Professor Saloninus and buy him a drink. He must be really smart."

"Smartest man who ever lived," I said automatically. "Only he's dead. He must be," I added, "because it was ninety-odd years ago. My professor Saloninus must be someone else with the same name."

"Not necessarily. Depends on just how smart he really is. Anyhow, that's not important right now. What's important is, I have a plan, and you're not to worry your pretty little head about it. And now I want you to go outside and have another talk with your friend."

"No," I said.

He looked at me. One short swing and he could smash my face so badly I'd be in pain for the rest of my life. I've often wished I could hit like that, only I suspect the skill would come at too high a price. "Fine," he said. "You know what? I trust you. I think you believe you're in so much trouble with Him it really doesn't matter anymore, so what the hell? I won't be long. Mind the angel."

He disappeared up the ladder. I counted to fifty, then I turned to face her.

"How would it be," I said, "if you and I made a deal?"

She looked at me. "A deal."

"I let you out of here. You make it all right with Him."

She closed her eyes, thinking about it. "I'm not sure," she said. "I don't think I can promise that."

"Excuse me?"

A dreamy sort of look. "I don't think I can guarantee the safety of your immortal soul," she said. "In which case, if you helped me escape, I'd be obtaining a valuable benefit under false pretences. I can't do that, obviously. I don't think," she went on, "that you'll be forgiven, even if you help me escape. You see, you haven't done anything wrong."

I was so bewildered I wanted to hit her. "So?"

"So if you've done nothing wrong, you can't be forgiven, can you? Nothing to forgive. But your grandfather did plenty. And because the sins of the fathers are visited upon the sons to the third or fourth generation—"

"That's not fair."

"I never said it was, but it's the law. And your grandfather never repented, so there can be no forgiveness. Sorry about that, but there it is."

I didn't understand. "That doesn't make sense," I said. "Presumably my grandfather's in hell right now, paying for what he did to you, so why should I have to?"

"Not necessarily." She could have been discussing art history, or minutiae of textual scholarship. "I can't say, because I've been stuck in here out of touch and I don't know what happened to him. But if He's taking it out on you, I'm guessing your grandfather was forgiven, even though he didn't repent. In which case there's a debt outstanding and someone's got to pay, and that person would logically be you. Just speculation," she added. "But that's how things work."

"You're not making any sense," I managed not to shout. "If he was forgiven, he must have repented."

"Not necessarily." She liked that phrase. "He could easily have been forgiven on some other grounds. Charity, good works, a sudden outburst of compassion leading to a good deed, which covered a multitude of sins. That's entirely plausible, you'd be surprised how often that happens. Or maybe someone really, really good prayed for him and he got off the hook that way. In which case," she went on, "he'd be in the clear and you'd be left holding the baby. And before you say it, yes, that's totally unfair, but that's how it goes. Compassion and forgiveness are the opposite of justice, when you come to think of it."

I felt like I'd been hit over the head with an iron bar. In case you think I'm being fanciful, it happened to me once, by accident. The pain was really, really bad, but worse was the not being able to think, for about five minutes. That's a very long time, in context. "So I'm screwed," I said.

"Yes," she said. "I think that more or less sums it up."

"Because of my grandfather."

"Yes, basically. At least you can comfort yourself with the thought that it wasn't your fault. I know, small comfort. But there you go."

"But that's crazy," I said. "What in God's name did he do?"

She looked at me. "You mean you don't know?"

"Obviously." I hesitated. "I thought it was all just stories."

She thought for a moment. "Strictly speaking," she said, "you don't need to know, so I shouldn't tell you. But since He can't hear us, what the heck. I'll tell you. Better still, I'll show you."

I didn't like the sound of that. "Please," I said, "don't go to any trouble. A brief summary will do just fine. And Florio'll be back any minute, so if we're going to get you out of here—"

"It's no bother at all," she said with a certain blood-in-the-water relish. "It was like this."

~

Vision, dream, maybe a form of memory buried deep in the marrow, I don't know; I was my grandfather, and I was standing on a chair. There was a rope round my neck. The other end was tied to a beam. I knew where I was, because I hadn't moved. Back then, of course, the chapel hadn't been built over it; I was in the root cellar of a derelict farmhouse.

I looked round to see if I could see who was lynching me. I was alone.

And why not, I thought; if I hang my grandfather before he has a chance to kidnap the angel, then the bad stuff won't happen and I won't end up carrying the can for it. Of course, by the same token I won't ever get to be born; but that's no bad thing, because if I never live, I can't get sent to eternal torment. I looked down. I could see the tips of my toes, balancing on a basic three-legged milking stool. Not the most stable of platforms at the best of times. I had no idea what had depressed my grandfather enough to make him want to end it all, but doubtless he had his reasons. Probably I'd be doing him a favour; and if not (definitely not, since he went on to be rich and powerful and even escaped punishment for his sins, the jammy bastard) then no matter; I'd be the one escaping. I could feel everything: the rope, the chair under my feet, the sweat trickling down the bridge of my nose. I tried wiggling my toes, which I doubt very much my grandfather did at this point in his career. They wiggled. Not, therefore, a vision, dream, or form of memory. This was real. I was under my own control. I could hang myself (and my grandfather), change history and cheat eternal torment of a customer by not being born, if I looked sharp about it.

Ay, but to die and go we know not where, to lie in cold obstruction and to rot. On the other hand; not my body, not my life, I'd never exist so I'd never suffer—

The hell with it, no pun intended.

How do you go about hanging yourself, exactly? They say, kick away the stool, but it's not easy to kick something when you're standing on it. If you lift one foot to kick with, your whole weight rests on the other, pinning the stool securely to the ground. If you jump with both feet, all that happens is that you land again a split second later; I know, because I tried and that's what happened. What I needed to do was find some way of deliberately overbalancing—

A man was standing there, looking at me. I recognised him, of course, even though he was a total stranger and my grandfather had never set eyes on him before. "Sorry," he said, "I'm intruding. I'll go away."

"Thanks," I tried to say, but the rope round my neck made it come out as a sort of gurgle.

He turned away, then turned back. "Look," he said, "I know it's none of my business, but you clearly haven't thought this through."

"Really, I—"

"For a start," he said, "that knot's completely wrong. You've used a bow hitch, when what you want is a running slipknot or something of the sort that'll tighten when you pull on it. Also that's a sisal rope, which is soft and springy. You want hemp for that job, it's dense and doesn't stretch, that's why it's the industry standard. And your drop—" He did a sort of words-fail-me shrug. "There's a reason why hangman is a skilled profession," he said. "I just hate to see people doing things all wrong, that's all. Excuse me. I'll go now."

"Just a minute," I said.

He sighed. "Fine," he said. "Look, if you go ahead, there's too much give in the rope and your knot's all wrong, and because your drop's too short you won't get enough pressure on the windpipe and what pressure you do get won't be properly distributed. You'll dangle there being just about able to breathe until someone comes and cuts you down, but by then your neck'll be a total mess, and cutting off the supply of blood to large areas of the brain is never a good idea, so you'll spend the rest of your possibly quite long life as a helpless drooling cripple. I don't know the first thing about you, but no matter how bad things may be right now, what you're about to do is likely to make them ever so much worse. Not, as I said, that it's any of my business. I just thought I'd mention it, that's all."

Suddenly I felt extremely nervous; one false move and the consequences didn't bear thinking about. "Help me," I squeaked. "Please."

He sighed. "Fact is," he said, "I'm late for a very important appointment on the far side of town."

"Please."

He rolled his eyes. "Fine," he said. "Stay there, don't move. Leave everything to me. Why is it," he added, "that whenever you really need a penknife, you leave it in your other trousers?"

It took what seemed like a very long time for him to cut the rope. I guess that was because he did it the best possible way, as you'd expect from Saloninus, the smartest man in the world. It couldn't be him, obviously. But it was, and not a day older, or younger, than when I'd seen him last, a week ago. I could only assume my grandfather's memory was playing tricks on me. Payback, for me trying to kill him.

"Right," he said, "you can get down off the stool now. That's it, easy does it." He steadied me with a gentle hand on my elbow. "Now then," he went on, "if you're still hell-bent on suicide, I recommend a good, reliable poison. Aconite's good, and there's always hemlock, though the variety that grows round here isn't the right sort. What you need is the kind with the purply leaves and the little sprays of white flowers."

"Thanks," I said, "but I don't think I'll bother."

"You sure? Look, if it's the uncertainty that's worrying you, how about jumping off a tall building? We've got a bell tower back at the University that's nearly three hundred feet, and there's a staircase all the way to the top. The sacristan's a friend of mine, he'd lend me the key."

"I think I'll live," I said. "Thanks all the same."

He shrugged. "If that's what you want," he said. "In that case, I suggest you go and have a good stiff drink." He looked at me, something that I hadn't been able to do, obviously. "Got any money?"

I put my hand in my pocket. "No," I said.

He clicked his tongue. "I thought not. Frittered away your last few trachy on unsuitable rope, I wouldn't be surprised. Tell you what," he said. "Do a small job for me and I'll pay you a hundred trachy."

Quick mental calculation; in my grandfather's day, enough to feed a man for a week, if he didn't object to stale bread. "What sort of job?"

"Does it matter? You're the one with nothing left to live for."

Fair enough. "What do I do?"

"Piece of cake," he said. "You go into the Silver Curtain temple, you know, just off Foregate. You go to the Trinity chapel, which is just inside the main door and turn left through a little arch. On the left hand side as you go in, on the wall at about shoulder height, there's a small icon of the Transfiguration, about yay big. Take it down off the wall and go to the Seven Stars in Sheep Street. In the chimney corner you'll find a bald man in a blue coat. Give him the icon, then come back here, a hundred trachy."

I looked at him. "That's stealing from a temple," I said. "That's really bad."

"Oh come on," he said. "Would I ask you to do a thing like that? No, it's my icon, I gave it to the temple, but it needs cleaning. The bald man is a professional picture restorer. I'd do it myself, but I've got this very important appointment in Chapelgate, for which I'm now going to be late because I stopped to save your life. Really I'm inventing a job as an excuse for giving you money without offending your pathetic dignity."

Put like that, how could I possibly refuse? "All right," I said.

"Splendid. Meet me in Chapelgate under the arches and I'll give you the hundred."

Outside, the clouds had passed over and the sun had come out. On my way to the temple, I paused to look at myself in a puddle. I was a mess: dirty, torn clothes; hair greasy and knotted; thin, drawn face from not enough food; hard to imagine this piece of human rubbish going on to be so very rich and respectable. I knew where the Silver Curtain was, but I'd never been in there before; the first time in my life, in fact, that I'd had a chance to see objects of exquisite beauty. I stood and gawped for a long time before remembering what I'd come for. Then I found the icon, took it and walked down the hill to Sheep Street.

"Out," said the landlord. "We don't need your kind in here."

"I'm not stopping," I said. I saw the bald man. "I've got something for that man there."

The bald man took the icon without looking at it; I left him to his drink and hurried back up the hill to Chapelgate. The professor was there waiting for me, sitting on the steps, reading a book.

"All done?" he said.

"Yes. Can I have my money?"

"Sure." He put his hand in his sleeve and took out a little cloth purse. It was about the right size. "Well," he said, "best of luck. If ever you're passing the University, look me up and tell me how you're getting on. My name's Saloninus."

No, I wanted to tell him, it's not, it can't be. "Thanks," I said.

"No problem," he said, and walked away.

A hundred trachy; food, maybe even a bed for the night. Clearly my grandfather had been given a second chance through the kind intervention of a stranger. It'd be criminally irresponsible of me to squander any of it on drink, even though my throat felt like the bottom of a dried-up well. I opened the purse and spilled the coins out onto my hand.

They were gold, not copper. A hundred staurata.

I knew—whether my grandfather would've known at that point in his career is another matter—that the icon I'd taken from the temple was worth about four hundred staurata; a vast, staggering sum to most people. One hundred, a quarter, was what a thief would expect to get from a fence. I couldn't make any sense of it. I sat down on a bench and stared at the money. I was still staring at it when the Watch came and arrested me.

"That's him," the bald man told them, down at the Watch house. "He gave it to me. I'd know him anywhere."

He was clearly a respectable citizen, because they

took his word over mine without a moment's hesitation. On the way to the cells I told the Watch captain that professor Saloninus from the University paid me to do it. I don't think he believed me.

"Can I ask you something?" I said to the man who brought me my bread and water the next morning. "What's the penalty for stealing from a temple?"

"They string you up," he said. "Why?"

"Just curious."

What I couldn't make out was why Saloninus (the smartest man who ever lived) should spend a hundred trachy of presumably his own money to bring about a result that would've happened anyway, unless he hadn't been telling the truth about the unsuitability of sisal rope. Made no sense. Still, I thought, as I nibbled the stale bread, looked at logically it really made no odds. I was back where I'd started from, poised to escape the horrific consequences of my grandfather's crime. In another man's body in another time, it would've been easy to lose sight of the big issue—eternal torment in hellfire, let's not forget about that for one moment. But if that was going to happen, surely that implied that the angel, by bringing me there, was letting me off the hook. Well, of course. If my grandfather got hung for stealing from a temple, he couldn't kidnap any angels. Perfect.

"On your feet," said the jailer.

I looked at him. "Excuse me?"

"Out of here," he explained. "We need the space."

It had all been, Saloninus was telling the captain when I got there, a silly misunderstanding. At the time when the alleged theft was taking place, he'd been talking to this poor homeless man in Chapelgate. Yes, he was absolutely certain it was the same man. I was completely innocent. Of course, professor, and it was incredibly noble and public-spirited of you to traipse all the way down here and explain just to save the life of this slab of trash. Just sign here, here and here and you can be on your way.

"I don't understand," I said, as we walked across the square.

"Of course you don't," said the professor. "You look like you could use a drink. Here," he added, as we sat down at a table in the Flawless Diamonds of Orthodoxy in Cutters Row, "you forgot to pick up your money."

"What money?"

"Your hundred staurata."

"Not my money."

He gave me an oh-come-on look. "I could hardly tell them it was mine, now could I? Besides, it is your money. You earned it."

I shrugged. "I got out of there with my neck the same length it was when I went in," I said. "That'll do me. What the hell is going on? Why did you—?"

He put the cloth purse down on the table. "I picked it up for you. Go on, take it." I didn't move. He scowled. "That's a lot of money," he said, "enough to give you the most amazing start in life. Take it."

Put like that; presumably my grandfather had at some point acquired a most amazing start in life; presumably this was it. I took it and dropped it in my pocket. "Thanks," I said. "I think."

He beamed at me. "Can you write?"

I remembered who I was. "No."

"In that case," he said, producing a scrap of paper and a stub of charcoal, "just scrawl a cross there, where my finger is. It's only a receipt, to show you've taken the money."

Here I was in a dilemma. I had far too much sense to sign a bit of paper I hadn't read under circumstances like those, but my grandfather? My guess was, he had more sense but probably wouldn't have given a damn; if the loony wants a cross scrawled, scrawl him a cross, because this time tomorrow I'll be miles away under an assumed name. I scrawled a cross. He folded the paper up and put it in his sleeve. "Thank you," he said. "Now it's all done, dusted, and official. Beer?"

I don't like beer. My grandfather almost certainly did. "Sure," I said. "You didn't answer my question."

"Beer first. It's sort of an article of faith with me."

It wasn't very nice beer. "Now," I said. "Tell me what all this is about. Please."

He smiled. There was a foam moustache on his upper lip, which he licked away with the tip of his tongue. "Simple," he said. "You stole an icon. From a temple. That's bad."

I looked at him. "You what?"

"And accepted money for doing so," he went on, "even after you knew that what you'd done was stealing. That's a mortal sin. From now on, your soul isn't worth—" He took out a silk handkerchief and spat into it "—that."

It took a moment for all that to sink in. "So all this was to damn me to hell?"

"Yes." He raised a hand. "I wouldn't bother with violence: you'll just make things worse for yourself. You're completely and utterly screwed, and only I can save you. But I can't do that if you tear my throat out, now can I?"

"You arsehole," I said. "How could you do a thing like that? What harm did I ever—?"

"Irrelevant," he said. Then he lowered his voice and

leaned a little closer. "Besides, I didn't steal the icon, you did. I haven't done anything, except save your life, twice. The fact is," he said, "I'm engaged in the single most important scientific experiment in the history of the world. If I succeed, it'll mean an unimaginably better future for all mankind. You're probably all right, no better and no worse than most people, but with stakes like that to play for, you simply don't matter worth shit. And neither do I," he added pleasantly, "and I'm the smartest man who ever lived. Nothing matters except the experiment. It's that important."

How my grandfather managed to control his temper at this point I had no idea. I only managed it because I knew he had. "What do you mean by *only I can save you*?" I said. "If you're right and I've committed a mortal sin—"

"Just a moment," he said. "You believe, don't you?"

"What sort of a question is that? Of course I do." Because I've met Him, I didn't add, and tried not to think about how my grandfather had answered the question. "Of course I believe. What do you take me for, an idiot?"

"Fine," he said. "Do you like Him?"

"What?"

"Do you like Him? God."

"*Like—*"

He nodded. "That's right. I don't mean love, fear, adore, revere. Do you like God? Based on what you know of Him, do you think He's a nice guy and the sort of person you'd be friends with, if you got to know Him socially?" He leaned forward a little bit. "More to the point, do you approve of the way He goes about things?"

I opened my mouth, closed it again, thought and said, "No, not really."

"Me neither." He smiled. "I think He's horrible. He's self-righteous, always assumes He knows best about everything, incredibly judgemental, harsh, cruel, down on you like a ton of bricks over the least little thing. Oh, He'll forgive you, if you sincerely repent and come grovelling, but that's just another way of saying that unless you see things a hundred per cent His way, you're eternal firewood. Anyway, that's not the point. What if you haven't done anything wrong? Take you, for instance. Did you do anything wrong?"

"No."

"Yes you did, you stole an icon from a temple. And clearly you aren't truly repentant, because you just said, no, you didn't do anything. Why did you steal from a temple?"

Good question. "I thought it was all right. You told me—"

"Oh come on," he said. "You didn't believe all that. You knew it was stealing, but you wanted the money. Needed the money," he added, "because you were starving. Why were you starving? Was it because you're a wicked, evil man who doesn't deserve food or a dry place to sleep? I don't think so. If you stole, it was because He made you do it. He created a world that condemned you to be a starving criminal from the day you were born. And then He turns round and damns you to hell for lifting a bit of painted wood off a wall." He paused, and smiled. "You know what? I don't like Him very much. I believe in Him, the same way I believe in war and earthquakes and bubonic plague, but I don't like Him. I think He's a hypocrite and a bully, and it's high time we started fighting back."

I rolled my eyes. "But we can't—"

"Yes." His smile turned fierce, like the sun. "We can. Or I can, at any rate." Another pause, just enough to drive me crazy. "Want to hear about it?"

So he told me about the room he was building. All the math went over my head like a flock of migrating geese, but there was a point in time, mayfly-brief and substantial as the last fleeting fragment of a dream when you wake up, when I think I understood, more or less, what he was talking about. A room where you could shut out God; a room where He doesn't exist.

"Which is fine," Saloninus went on, "if spending the rest of your life in a root cellar is your idea of fun. It's not mine. So we need a way of using it as a weapon."

"A weapon? Are you nuts?"

Sigh. "Timidity," he said. "Cowardice. A luxury you could afford if you weren't going straight to hell. Think of it," he said, "as a jailbreak. You've smashed a hole in the wall, well done, clever you. But you don't just sit there waiting for the guards to show up, you run. Well, here's our hole in the wall. We need to get moving."

False premise there somewhere, but my grandfather wouldn't have known a false premise from a stick of rhubarb, so I let it pass. "A weapon," I said, "means picking a fight. With Him. I don't want to do that."

"He started it. And you're in a fight already." He grinned at me, like a wolf. "I don't think you'll enjoy Hell," he said. "Especially the fire. Did you ever get burned? Well, think what it felt like, and it never stops. Not ever. For all time. My guess is," he went on, "He designed the body and the nervous system so that burning is the worst possible pain that can happen to you. Deliberately, so as to make it suitable for the punishment. Now, what sort of a person would do a thing like that?"

My head was buzzing. If there's one fundamental rule

of life, it's that you can't fight the authorities. But what if you could? An intoxicating thought even under normal circumstances. For a man damned to hell—

(Hold on a moment, I thought. Didn't the angel just tell me that my grandfather didn't get damned to hell, which was why He was after me to pay off the unpaid bill? In which case, I knew that Saloninus' scheme was going to work, had already worked, therefore—)

"What the fuck," I said. "You really think you can do it?"

He grinned at me, and I had an uneasy feeling that he knew what had just passed through my mind; not telepathy or magic, but because somehow he *remembered*—Did he know who I really was? Impossible. But so's fighting God. "It's simple math," he said. "I did the equations. I checked them twice. It works."

I indulged myself in a long sigh. "You've got a plan, haven't you?"

He nodded. "And all we need," he said, "is a monk."

No problem. The city's crawling with them.

There are many different sorts of monk, needless to say. There's the rich ones, who own practically everything—the docks, the freighters, the grain mills, the turnpikes, the smithies, the mines, the quarries, the sawmills, the weirs, the water towers, the brickyards, the limekilns, everything you need but can't afford to build for yourself. There's a lot of them, and they wouldn't give the likes of my grandfather the time of day; unfortunate, since they own all the clocks. Then there's the poor ones; the mendicant orders, the poor friars, who preach on street corners with a wooden bowl at their feet. Both sorts are men of genuine piety, unimpeachably sincere, but the friars are easier to get at.

"Excuse me," I said, "but are you busy right now?"

Brother Chrysostom looked up at me. He hadn't eaten for a week and he stank. "No, not really," he said. "Can I help you?"

"It's like this," I said. I explained that my employer, a wealthy eccentric, had built a ruined priory—

"A *ruined*—"

I nodded. "It's been built ruined," I said, "because of being romantic and artistic. I told you, he's eccentric. Anyhow, he's built it and now he needs a hermit."

He frowned. "Why would anyone need a hermit?"

"To look good," I said. "Ruined priory, complete with hermit. Nobody else has got one, so he wants one. Screw him," I said. "The point is, he'll give you food and shelter and a place where you can pray in peace and quiet, and he'll also give two hundred staurata to the poor. That's got to be a good deal. Everyone's a winner."

He was thinking so hard I could feel the ground tremble under my feet. "He wants me to pray for his soul."

"Only if you feel like it. You don't have to pray *for* anything. You've just got to pray. And be picturesque, of course, though there won't be anyone to see you."

"There won't? In that case, what's the point?"

"He'll know you're there," I said. "And so will everybody he tells about you. Meanwhile," I went on, lowering and sweetening my voice, "you can pray your socks off in absolute peace and quiet and still be doing a shitload of good for the poor and needy. What's not to like about that?"

What indeed? So Brother Chrysostom came with me to the newly built ruined priory, underneath which was a root cellar. I asked him what he liked to eat; barley bread, he said, and a few onions. I fetched them. When you want some more, I said, raise the flag on the flagpole. Then I left him to it.

In the trade, as I think I've told you already, we call it an epiphany. I'd done my homework and chosen Brother Chrysostom with great care; thirty years living on the streets, praying, helping people, looking after the sick, by example, nothing to show for it apart from hollow cheeks, chilblains, sores from lying on hard pavements, and a buildup of potential grace so massive it could bend sunlight. The smart money said he was a dead certainty for an epiphany any day now. All I had to do was make sure it happened in the freshly ruined priory—

The next few weeks were utterly miserable for me. I spent them crouched in a corner behind a stack of empty barrels, hardly daring to breathe in case I made a noise and gave away the fact that I was there hiding, my fingers numb from gripping the end of a piece of string. If that wasn't bad enough, I had to put up with the endless repeated chanting—the Benedicite, the Mundus Vergens, the Psalms Ordinary and Occasional, the Dimitte Nobis, all that. The bit of string was tied to a latch. Naturally I couldn't relax for a split second, just in case it happened while my attention was wandering.

Which of course it was, when the moment eventually came; I'd fallen into a doze, and it was only the brilliance of the light that woke me up. It was so bright it burnt my face and I daren't look to see if the angel was directly on top of the trapdoor or not. I just had to hope, which is a way of saying I had to have faith. Fuck it, I muttered to myself, and pulled the string.

~

(Now that was one variable Saloninus hadn't been able to calculate. When the trapdoor gave way, would the angel fall through, subject to the laws of something or other, or would she float in midair and give me a reproachful look? It all depended on whether the trapdoor was technically part of the God-free room—like an embassy theoretically being foreign soil—or whether it was just a piece of hinged wood. He'd done the math one way and it came out as a positive. Then he tried a different approach and got a negative; so much for the absolute objective truth of science. "Fingers crossed," he'd said to me, after we'd tested the latch mechanism for the fifth time. Wonderful.

—Because it was my immortal neck on the line, not his; that's why I was there. Saloninus had planned everything, we'd discussed everything, *inside the room*, where He couldn't hear us. As far as He knew, all this was my wicked, sinful idea and Saloninus was as pure as the driven snow. So if I pulled the string and the angel floated, I'd be the one who tried to kidnap an angel, I'd be the one who spent eternity as sustainable solid fuel—which I'd be doing anyway, because of stealing from a temple; entirely my idea to do that, because our conversation had taken place in the room ... Smartest man who ever lived? Yes, I'd go along with that.)

~

I pulled the string. There was a shriek. The angel vanished. I let go of the string and the trapdoor (thanks to a complex system of balances and counterweights) slammed back into place. Job done.

Brother Chrysostom was looking at me. "What just happened?" he said.

It's a sin to tell a lie. "Don't ask me," I said.

~

In those days there was a back way into the root cellar; I had it bricked up shortly afterwards, apparently. I hurried down and found Saloninus and the angel facing each other like two cats. She was small, slight and frail-looking, but she had a sword; under normal circumstances it would have been flaming, but even a non-flaming sword is a factor to be reckoned with in a confined space. I snuck up behind her and kicked it out of her hand. Round one, therefore, to the mortals.

"Quick," Saloninus yelled at me. "Break her wings."

"You *what*?"

"Do it." So I did it. You know how it is. Have you ever killed a chicken? Me, no; my grandfather, loads of times, invariably chickens that properly speaking belonged to somebody else. The risk is, when pulling their necks, that you pull too hard. A gentle tug and the chicken carries on thrashing and squawking, which makes you feel terrible. You increase the pressure a modest degree. The stupid head comes off in your hand. Turns out it's the same with angels; no middle ground, so to speak. I stood there for a moment with a wing in my hand, and silvery blood, like mercury, dripping on my shoes. Pulling the wings off angels, for crying out loud; and the silly thing was, it wasn't a crime and I hadn't done anything wrong (not yet) because *nobody knew*—

"You clown," Saloninus said. "Still, not to worry. Now the other one. *Gently*, this time."

"Fuck you," I said.

He sighed. "Right now," he said, "we're in uncharted territory. There are certain things we don't know about angels. We know how many of them can dance on the head of a pin, but not whether they can fly effectively on one wing. Break the other one. Now."

Second time lucky. You use both hands and press inward with the thumbs. Piece of cake.

~

"That's what happened," she said.

I looked up. "Who am I?" I said.

She grinned at me. "You're you," she said, "not your grandfather. Welcome back to your nasty and unsatisfactory life."

"Thanks," I said. "Now beat it. Get out of here, before he comes back."

She raised an eyebrow. "Compassion?" she said. "Or just guilt?"

"Go away," I said. "Please."

"Sorry," she said, "I can't do that. Not without wings. I can't walk, you see."

"What?"

"I can't walk, I can only fly." Sad smile. "My legs don't actually work, they're just for show. When you see an angel apparently walking, she'd be hovering a quarter of an inch above the ground. Without wings, I can't leave. Physically impossible. I'm not entirely sure why He made us like that, but presumably there was a reason."

Oh for crying out loud. "That's all right," I said. "I'll carry you."

"You can try if you like."

I tried. She weighed a ton. With all my strength and all my might, I just about managed to get her off the floor; then my back gave way and I dropped her. I collapsed, doubled up with pain, bright spots flashing in front of my eyes, barely able to breathe. "Sorry," she said. "But in here, with no God to help you, you're constrained by the parameters of the possible. Of course, the fact that you even tried would count heavily in your favour if only He could have seen it. But He can't, so it was all a waste of time and effort."

I scowled at her. "You're not helping," I said. Forcing the words out hurt. "Do you want to get out of here or not?"

"Do I *want*—?" Blank look. "You don't understand about us, do you? It's not up to me. Are you really a theology student? Only you don't seem to know a whole lot about theology."

I sat down. I was just starting to get my breath back. "One thing you didn't tell me."

"Really? What was that?"

"Saloninus. His experiment. Did it work?"

She shrugged. "How would I know? I've been in here all the time, cut off. I was going to ask you the same question, except that would be curiosity, a sin of which I'm not capable. But in here it wouldn't matter—" She smiled. "But you don't know the answer, so I won't demean myself by asking the question."

I thought about it for a moment. Had Saloninus ever actually said what the experiment was? To build a room where you could be free of God—yes, but he'd already done that before he met my grandfather. To kidnap an angel? No point to that, on its own; the point would be the ransom. The angel was still palpably here, which suggested that no ransom had ever been paid, no deal ever struck. In which case, how come my grandfather wasn't in hell? "I don't suppose," I asked nicely, "you know how the story ended."

She looked at me. "The story never ends," she said. "I'd have thought you'd have known that, being a theologian."

Just then, Florio came tumbling down the ladder. His face was red and shining, like he'd been working in a furnace, and he was so excited he couldn't keep still.

"I had a chat," he said, "with your pal. He's all right, actually, when you get to know Him."

"He's not my pal," I said. "All right, what did He say?"

Florio was looking for something to drink. He found the water jug but it was empty. "No problem," he said. "Turns out I'm the long-lost heir to the throne of Chosroene. Perfectly legitimate," he added, as I pulled a face, "because nobody ever had a clue who my dad was, but apparently this birthmark I've got on my left shoulder is absolutely, what's the word, incontrovertible." He pulled his shirt down so I could see. "And the old king just abdicated to join a monastery, and the grand vizier's on his way here to find me, after spending ten years tracking me down." He paused and frowned. "So presumably He can do stuff retrospectively."

She nodded. "Standing on His head," she said. "But you always were the king's son. You just didn't know it."

"Figures. Anyhow, the vizier knows all about it because he's seen me in a dream, and he's going to make all the arrangements. This time tomorrow I'll be on a ship to Chosroene to start my new life. Thirty-five years of absolute power. It doesn't get much better than that."

The angel gave him a thin smile. "Congratulations," she said.

He ignored her. "Meanwhile," he went on, "I haven't forgotten what I said. You get to be governor of Buciris. Never been there, obviously, but they say it's the earthly paradise."

"That's nice," I said. "What about her?"

"What about her? She stays here, obviously. All we need is a new flagstone for the trapdoor. You might see to that, while we're waiting for the vizier to show up."

I glared at him. "I'm not going out there," I said. "It's not safe."

"Don't talk stupid. Of course it's safe. I fixed every-thing, remember?"

"For you," I said. "I'm the one who'll be left carrying the can. That's what I'm here for."

He gave me a funny look. "Bullshit," he said. "Would I do that to you, my right hand man? We're in this to-gether, so where I go, you go. I fixed it for you, with your mate."

I closed my eyes. "What have you done?"

"You get thirty-five years, same as me," he said cheer-fully. "Oh come on. Ask anyone. They'll tell you. Florio never leaves anyone behind. It's the rule. That's how people know they can trust me."

I thought about his dead cousins in the room over-head. "You shouldn't have bothered," I said. "Really."

"No bother at all." He stopped and listened. Someone was moving about upstairs. "That'll be the vizier," he said. "Efficiency, I like that. Pull yourself together, for crying out loud. This is going to be a blast."

I didn't comment, because obviously Florio hadn't thought it through. If the angel was telling the truth (how the hell would she know, if she'd been isolated for all of Florio's life?), Florio had always been the rightful king, in which case he'd have come into his inheritance in due course without any need to abduct or illegally detain angels . . . So wasn't it a bit of a coincidence that his ambition (to be achieved by criminal methods) just happened to coincide with his birthright? But an angel can't tell a lie; therefore, if she knew, she must've known *before* the abduction—

"I need some time," I said. "There's someone I want a word with."

"Don't be stupid. We need to go now."

"I won't be long," I said. "You stay here and chat to the vizier. I expect you'll have a lot to talk about."

Normally he'd have smashed my face in, to maintain his dignity, but I could see he had other things on his mind. I stepped past him and scrambled up the ladder.

Outside it was bright sunshine, which made me shudder, bearing in mind what it was and where it came from. I'd never properly considered it in that light, no pun intended, before. The mere presence of the Supreme Being is enough to grow wheat and keep us warm and able to cross a field without bumping into trees. What did God ever do for me? The answer is all around you, except at night. Annoying in a way that I'd come to that pretty essential piece of knowledge by the act of cutting myself off from it; like someone who lives a thousand miles inland proving the existence of the sea by drowning in it. Never mind. I glanced up at the sun, but only to give myself an approximate idea of the time. Shortly before noon. If I ran, I could just about make it.

~

"You're late," said Professor Saloninus. Needless to say, he's got a clock. It's a real clock, not a sundial; springs and cogs and ratchets, he made it himself with a lathe and lots of little sharp files, presumably so there'd be one less thing he had to rely on the sun for. And his time would always be objectively accurate, entirely and absolutely man-made, provided he remembered to keep the thing wound up.

"Sorry, professor," I said, sinking into a chair. "And I haven't done the essay on moral relativism."

He peered at me. "Ah," he said.

"Actually." I took a deep breath. "There's something important I want to ask you. Did you know my grandfather?"

His face froze, and he nodded.

"She's still there."

He breathed in long and slow; that centering thing, I assume. "I know," he said. "Did your grandfather ever tell you about the experiment?"

"He died before I was born. But that's what I wanted

to ask you about."

He didn't speak for a moment. Instead he drummed his fingers on his knees, like someone playing an invisible clavichord. "Your grandfather," he said, "kidnapped an angel."

"Because you tricked him into it."

He nodded. "Before we go any further," he said, "you probably ought to know that the chapel cellar isn't unique. When I knew it worked, I used the same technology here, in my study."

"I see," I said. "So that's why the blinds are always drawn."

He smiled. "Quite," he said. "No point going to all that trouble if He could simply peek in through the window. I can't tell you about the experiment, I'm afraid."

"Why the hell not?"

"Observer effect." He frowned. "Actually, more like participant effect. It's still running and you're part of it. If you know about it, that could spoil everything."

My turn for a couple of deep breaths. "I see," I said. From inside my coat I produced a knife I'd borrowed from a dead goon on the way out of the chapel. "Here's the deal," I said. "You tell me what I want to know and I won't cut your throat."

He grinned. "You've been spending too much time with Florio," he said. "But not enough to have learned how to do it properly. A threat from him I'd have to take seriously. From you, on the other hand—"

His arm moved, very fast. I saw a blinding light and then I was on the floor. My head hurt unbearably.

"Sorry," said the professor. He reached out and helped me up and I sat back in the chair, feeling sick. "Was that magic, do you think?"

"I don't know," I said.

"Actually, it wasn't." He opened his hand and showed me what was in it; a steel ball, the size of a small walnut. "I spend an hour a day practising," he went on. "Over longer ranges it's useless, but at ten feet, if you hit precisely the right spot—" He opened a cupboard, put my knife inside and locked it. "You may have a slight concussion. If so, it's your own fault. Florio would have ducked in time. He's got the reflexes, you see, after a lifetime of dealing with violent people."

"I'm sorry," I said.

"No you're not. But then, you shouldn't have to be. See my essay on true repentance in last year's *Theological Review*." He poured himself a drink of water from a jug on his desk. "I can't tell you about the experiment. But I can help you, if you'd like me to."

"You can?"

He nodded. "Can you stand?"

Just about, it turned out. "Where are we going?"

"Take care on the stairs. They can be tricky if your head's spinning."

One of those horrible spiral staircases, a long way down and no handrail. Eventually a door; inside the door, a room. Quite like the root cellar, but smaller and cleaner. In a corner of the room, a small stack of what looked like steel girders.

"In retrospect," said the professor, "it'd have been more sensible to build it at ground level. Getting all that up those stairs is going to be a bitch."

It was, he explained, a portable angel cage; or at least the components thereof, some assembly required. He gave me a sheet of paper with drawings, which he assured me was a complete set of instructions. "You put the framework together," he said, "and then cover it with black fabric. Linen, canvas, doesn't matter what, so long as it's black. It works on the same principles as the cellar and my study. For what it's worth, it's probably the cleverest thing ever made by man."

I looked at it. Lots of steel bars, with clamps. There was a cloth bag, presumably containing rivets. "You're right," I said. "We'll have to make several trips."

That got me a sour look. "It would be impossible," he said, "to put a price on something like this, in money. I don't think enough coins have been struck in the history of the world."

He wasn't fooling anyone. He'd built one, he could build another. This was just scaffolding. "It's the very least you could do," I pointed out. "Florio's going to be king of Chosroene."

He blinked. "Well, now," he said.

"I'm going with him. But now we can take the angel with us." I paused. "Will that screw up your experiment?"

"No." He smiled. "That's why I built the cage, in case of something like this. You can take the angel with you to—where did you say?"

"Chosroene."

He nodded slowly. "It would be," he said. "Any particular reason why Chosroene?"

My head was still hurting, especially when I used it to think. "Florio wanted to be king there. So he made that the ransom. Then it turned out that he was actually the rightful king all along."

"Of course it did." Saloninus picked up an armful of steel bars and thrust them at me. I managed to grab them without dropping one on my foot. "He's been set up. You do realise that."

"Excuse me?"

He sighed and loaded me down with more ironwork. "The Invincible Sun," he said, "rarely alters the past. Instead, He arranges things so as to give Himself an almost infinite variety of options. In other words, He sets people up. Don't you see? Florio is just an artefact, like you and me, a manufactured item, designed to perform certain functions; or at least be capable of performing them, should the need arise."

"Professor—"

"He was set up," Saloninus said. "Forty years ago the Invincible Sun ordained that the true king of Chosroene should be born and raised as a gangster. You wouldn't do that unless you're up to something."

Good point. I'd have appreciated it much more if the weight of the girders wasn't pulling my arms off. "The angel knew about it," I said.

That made him twitch an eyebrow; hot stuff. "Proves my point," he said. "She's been cut off from divine input for eighty-odd years, but she knows about it. Therefore it's part of the divine plan. Your friend Florio—"

"He's not my friend."

"Was born to commit the most atrocious sin imaginable. He had no choice. Do you know much about the law?"

"No. Would it be all right if I put this down for a moment?"

"Go ahead. In particular, the law relating to conspiracy; aiding, abetting and procuring a felony. Who is more guilty, the assassin or the man who hires him?" He shrugged. "I just thought I'd mention it. You can pick all that stuff up again now."

~

So we got some lifting equipment, packed the angel up in the cage, and off we went to Chosroene.

Interesting place. About ten percent of the population of the world live there, if you can call it living, with more people per acre than anywhere else on Earth. I think the climate is horrible—scorching hot most of the year, and the rest of the time it rains—but it makes for ideal growing conditions; wheat in the north, rice in the south, and there are huge fertile valleys gouged out of the mountains by the enormous rivers that carry all that incessant rainwater down to the sea. If seventy percent of its population were to drop dead overnight, Chosroene would be an earthly paradise for the survivors. As it is, the incredibly vast quantity of food produced there is only just enough to keep the incredibly enormous population fed, most but not all of the time.

For the overwhelming majority of Chosroenes life is mostly unbearable, leavened only by their devotion to their god-king. Every miserable palm leaf shack has a crude wooden doll, representing his ineffable majesty, in the place of honour. Every day, the best food in the house is put in front of it in a wooden bowl, and if his majesty's effigy isn't feeling peckish it cools down and is thrown out for the birds, because it'd be unthinkable for mere commoners to eat the king's share. The birds who eat the wasted food are sacred, because they feed on the king's leftovers. This means you get to see the uniquely Chosroene sight of beggars starving to death surrounded by whirring flocks of chubby sparrows and starlings, not to mention eminently edible pigeons; but nobody seems to mind, let alone conceive the thought that something might possibly be wrong. There's no law saying they have to do this, by the way; in fact, successive generations of kings have asked them not to. But they persist, because they want to. Sharing their dinner with the king is the only pleasure they have.

"This place," Florio said to me as we were carried on a litter through the streets of the capital, "is a shithole. Why in God's name did we ever come here?"

On either side of the street, soldiers were pushing people back with their spears held horizontally in both hands. I found out later that over a thousand died that morning, crushed or asphyxiated in their longing to see the king. But Chosroenes adore in silence; the loudest noises were the creaking of the spear-shafts, the clopping of hooves and Florio's voice, saying rude things about his birthright. The angel cage followed on behind us, also on a litter. Nobody had asked us what it was, and we hadn't volunteered any details.

The palace was enormous and probably the ugliest building I've ever seen in my life. Essentially it was a square stone box with a few narrow arrow-slits for windows; it made the State Penitentiary back home look like a fairy-tale castle, and it amused me to think that Florio had spent his entire life trying very hard to keep out of a rather more attractive dwelling than the one he'd sold our souls for. Inside the main gate it was different; not better, different. It was the same as the outside but covered in gold leaf. There were also frescoes, mosaics, and bas reliefs, pretty well everywhere you cared to look, all executed with gusto and total absence of taste in equal proportions. On balance, I preferred the outside, or the slums. They were equally depressing, but they didn't hurt your eyes quite so much when the sun shone.

"A sensible man," I said, as we hopped down off the litter in the central courtyard, "would've found out what it was like beforehand. It's horrible."

Florio shaded his eyes with his hand against the glare. "I'll have it all changed," he said. "Or maybe a new build, from scratch. Where's that vizier got to? The moment you take your eyes off him, he pisses off somewhere."

He's withdrawn because of respect. I didn't tell him; it didn't matter. The respect turned out to be a real nuisance, because there was nobody to tell us what to do. I'd been anticipating a tightly organised schedule; meetings with important people followed by audiences with foreign diplomats followed by sessions of the Privy Council and the treasury subcommittee, then the coronation, then whatever. None of that. No Chosroene would ever presume to make a suggestion to the king. Eventually we got the hang of it. Nothing happened unless we gave the order; once the order was given, they'd move heaven and earth to make sure it was carried out to the letter. Absolutely fine, assuming you know what you want—*everything* you want, from invading the neighbouring kingdom to having your chamber pot emptied. Anticipating the king's wishes would be blasphemy, since it implied that mere subjects might be capable of thinking on his level.

"I want to go home," I said.

"Me too," Florio said. "But fuck that. We'll just have to make this place how we want it. Hey, you," he said, to a man in a tall hat; I think he was the Lord Chamberlain. "Build me a new palace."

"Yes, majesty."

"I want an exact replica of the royal palace in Auxentia. And don't take forever over it." He turned to me. "What do you think? Five years? Five years should be plenty. Fetch me a map and I'll show you where I want it to be."

"Yes, majesty."

They brought him a map. "I think I'm getting the hang of this," Florio said.

The word *hang* reminded me of my grandfather. "I don't imagine you need me for anything," I said, "now you've come into your birthright. I think I may just head on home."

Being king hadn't meant Florio had lost his edge. His hand shot out and gripped my neck, thumb in the hole between the collarbones. "No," he said. "You stay right here."

The man in the tall hat and the other courtiers didn't seem to have noticed anything. At any rate, they didn't move a muscle. "But I don't want my reward," I said. "My reward sucks. And if you want to strangle me, fine."

"I need you," he said.

"What for?"

He increased the thumb pressure, and I realised I didn't need an answer to my question nearly as much as I needed air. "I see," I said, when he'd let me go. "Thank you for explaining."

"Any time."

~

A week in Chosroene as the second most important man in the kingdom and I really wished he'd throttled me after all. I might have coped better if I'd been able to spend at least some of the time on my own, but Florio wanted me there with him every minute of the day, so close that he could reach out and touch, hit, strangle me should he wish to do so; and he kept up an unceasing commentary, directed at me, about how horrible everything was and how he really didn't care for the way things were run and people smelt. Force of habit, I suppose, but he never quite turned his back on me, so even if I'd had the guts to stick a knife in him I wouldn't have had the chance. It would, of course, have been the last thing I ever did, but that wouldn't have bothered me all that much. If I died, I'd go straight to eternal torment; more or less the same experience, but almost certainly in less tiresome company.

"He's getting on your nerves, isn't he?" said the angel. I'd made it my principal duty to check up on her three times a day, not that it involved anything; the cage was padlocked, Florio had the only key, and she'd shown no inclination whatsoever to try and escape.

"Yes," I said.

"You want to try and be more charitable," she told me. "He's a part of the great scheme of being, just like you are. In fact, you're so alike it's hard to tell you apart sometimes."

"Don't say that, please."

She shrugged. "To the scythe, one stalk is much the same as another. I hope you're enjoying yourself, in spite of him. You really ought to cram in as much fun as you possibly can, considering."

I didn't need to ask, but I did. "Considering?"

"That in thirty-five years you're going to hell," she said sweetly. "One of the few privileges you're allowed in hell is memories, mostly because when you're there, memories aren't a privilege at all, they're part of the punishment. But you may care to assemble a portfolio of nice things to look back on when you're standing up to your waist in unquenchable fire."

"Only up to my waist," I said. "That's not so bad."

"Mondays, Wednesdays, and Fridays," she said. "And your top half's blasted by intolerably icy winds, so you burn and freeze at the same time. I probably shouldn't have told you that, because I'm not supposed to spoil the surprise, but since He can't hear me I don't suppose it matters. Apparently burning and freezing simultaneously sets up the most excruciating harmonics up and down the nerves. It's a case of the whole being more than the sum of its parts, if you get my drift."

"Have you actually been there?" I asked her.

"What me? Loads of times. Before I was an angel I was on the staff there. We do a rotation, you see, so many million years upstairs, so many million flip side. I'll be back down there again once I've finished this shift, so we'll be seeing a lot of each other in the future."

"Interesting," I said. "Angels and devils are the same people."

"One big happy divine family," she said. "World without end, amen. It's really helpful for your sense of perspective, and a change is as good as a rest." She yawned. "Sweet of you to pretend to take an interest, but it's not going to get you anywhere. I couldn't let you off the hook even if I wanted to."

"What about sincere repentance?"

"Oh come on, we've been over that already. You can't repent because you haven't done anything. You're on the hook because you're your grandfather's grandson. Somehow he managed to get away with it, so you've got to pay his tab." She gave me a sad look. "You can try repenting of the stuff you've actually done, but that won't do you the slightest bit of good, not in practice. Besides, you aren't sorry. You're just scared and unhappy because of the punishment. That's not the same thing at all. Really sorry means understanding the nature and quality of your actions and truly believing that those actions were morally wrong." Sigh. "That's the thing about belief, you can't make yourself do it. It's like falling asleep or being in love. You can lie there all night desperately wanting to go to sleep, and the more you want the more it doesn't happen. You can really, really want to believe, but if you don't you just don't."

"I used not to believe in Him," I said. "Until my nose got rubbed in the proof."

That made her smile. "Anomalous circumstances," she said. "Not something we usually allow. Anyhow, it's a different sort of belief. You see, He's a fact, like two and two making four. Loving your neighbour as yourself isn't, it's a state of mind. It depends on belief, you have to believe that it's the right thing to do, or it doesn't count. You clearly don't believe anything of the sort. Therefore you're screwed. But you were born screwed, so it really doesn't matter a tiny bit in the long run."

I closed my eyes, then opened them. "I look forward to our little chats," I said. "Only goes to show how totally shitty the rest of my life must be. Can't you say something cheerful and nice just once?"

She thought for a moment. "No," she said. "Sorry."

~

Florio is smart. Not in the way Saloninus is smart; Florio doesn't see the world as a great big machine to be taken to bits, understood, and put back together again in a rather more efficient configuration. Florio is essentially a predator. In his view, there are two categories; things you can eat, things that can eat you. He has nothing against either category; he doesn't make judgements. Occasionally he comes across anomalies, things that are neither opportunities nor threats, but I don't think they register with him somehow. It's like dogs; they can't see something properly unless it's moving. If Florio encounters something that doesn't fit in either of the two categories, he ignores it, and as far as he's concerned it might as well not exist, so to all intents and purposes it doesn't. The advantage of this way of seeing things is that it filters out all the irrelevant stuff, such as the scent of flowers and the sobbing of starving children, allowing him to concentrate with unabated ferocity on the things that matter to him. This makes him a highly efficient thinker, because he's not frittering away his energy and capacity on stuff that's none of his concern.

"We need to do something," he said to me, "about the poor."

Maybe I'd got wax in my ears. "Really?"

"You bet." We were leaning on the balcony of the top floor window, overlooking the street. One day a week there was a big market in the square. The country people came into town with things to sell and set up stalls, and the city people came to look at all the nice things they couldn't afford to buy. "Lots of people in this country don't have enough to eat. We need to fix that."

"Do we?"

He scowled at me. "Are you stupid or something? Of course we do."

"Ah."

"We need the farmers to grow more food," he said.

"And then we need to fix it so that everybody gets something, whether they can afford to pay or not. And a lot of the people who can't pay haven't got work to do. We ought to fix that. It's a waste, it's dumb. Actually, this whole country is a mess. It needs taking in hand."

I glanced over my shoulder at the angel cage. Florio hadn't been to look at her once since we got there; that was my job, mind the angel. So she hadn't been whispering sweet subversive nothings in his ear, not unless there was a leak in the professor's security, and he'd assured me on his honour as a genius that there couldn't be. "Just out of interest," I said. "Have you been hearing voices in your head lately?"

That got me a short left to the solar plexus, which I signally failed to see coming. Being around Florio had done wonders for my anticipatory skills, but I was still a long way short of being in his league. "Funny man," he said, as I sank to the floor. "And stupid. You're so lucky you've got me looking out for you."

Lucky, I thought, as I tried to suck air through crushed pipes. "Sorry," I mumbled.

"No you're not." He gave me an oh-for-pity's-sake look and helped me up. "You're dumb, is what you are. You never think."

If only that were true. "You've got a reason," I said.

"You bet." He guided me tenderly to a chair. "We're in the shit, you know that, don't you?"

I nodded.

"Just as well I've thought of a great way of digging us out again. We're going to feed the poor."

Ah, I thought. Silly of me. "You think we can buy our way out of hell with good works."

"Sure we can." He went away and came back with a sheaf of parchment. His handwriting is not at all what you'd expect; big letters, perfectly formed, perfectly spaced between lines ruled on the page with a lead pencil. A chaplain taught him to write when he was in jail, he told me; he never finished the lessons because he strangled the chaplain, stole his robes and escaped, but by then he'd learned the basics, so that's fine. "It's all down here," he said, shoving the parchment under my nose, so close it was all a blur. "The chancellor gave me the figures. How much stuff gets grown each year in each province, who owns all the land, how much money's in the treasury, all that. We can do it, easy. All it'll take is a few heads banging together."

Florio would be good at that. "They'll never stand for it," I said.

That made him grin. "Shows how much you know," he said.

As soon as I managed to get away from him, I consulted the angel. "Well?" I said.

She thought for a moment. "Actually," she said. "That's not a bad idea."

I was shocked. "That can't be right, surely."

"And you a theology student. Maybe you should've paid attention, instead of doodling in the margins of your textbooks." She paused to itch her shoulder against the bars of the cage. There was nothing to see yet, of course, but I had no doubt that the wings were already starting to grow back. "Doctrinally, it's perfectly sound. The Invincible Sun listens to the prayers of the righteous and grants them if they're morally valid. Now Florio is an evil sack of shit—" She paused and grinned. "I can say bad words as much as I like in here, isn't it fun? Florio's prayers will never be answered, because he's bad and he doesn't understand the nature and quality of his actions, so he can't sincerely repent. He knows that, that's fine. But the starving poor of Chosroene, several million of them—" She grinned. "You bet He's going to listen to them. If they all pray for the soul of the man who feeds and clothes them, fills the righteous up with good things and sends the rich empty away—" She shrugged; the gesture made her wince, because of the damage I'd done to the wing sockets. "Florio's motives are garbage," she said, "he's only doing it to save himself, so he gets no credit at all. But all those good, righteous people, all praying for his soul; I imagine He's got His lawyers working on it right now, just in case there's a loophole. But I can't see one myself. Mind you, I'm isolated from the group mind in here so I'm out of the loop."

"It can't work like that," I said. "It's unfair."

"Yes, it's unfair," she said. "Who ever said anything about it being fair? Mercy isn't fair, it means someone getting away with what he did because the Boss feels sorry for him. Justice is fair. Justice puts people in prison. Mercy lets them out again. Of course mercy isn't fair. It's breaking all the rules." She smiled at me. "Which one would you rather have, justice or mercy?"

"Yes, but—" Good point, I thought. "Even so," I said. "Florio's a *criminal*. God only knows how many people he's had murdered over the years."

"Yes," she said. "Of course He does."

"And beaten up, and robbed, and squeezed dry of every trachy they've got. Me for one. If it hadn't been for him, I wouldn't be—" I stopped. My grandfather's grandson.

I think she read my mind. "Yes," she said. "You would."

"And that's not fair either," I said. "I didn't do anything."

She nodded. "Yes you did," she said. "You *inherited*. Come on, then. Let's see the blisters on your hands, from all the hard days' work you've done in your life."

"That's different," I said. "I couldn't help being born. Nobody asked me."

"Quite," she said. "But you inherited, and then you accepted. You didn't renounce your unearned wealth and run away and start a soup kitchen in the slums of Choris. Of course you didn't. You just complained because it was quails eggs twice in a row for breakfast. I ask you, where's the justice in that?"

"And that's why I've got to burn in hell for something I didn't do. Where's the mercy in that?"

"No," she said patiently. "That's because you're your grandfather's grandson, we've been through it over and over again. I do wish you'd listen when I'm talking to you."

I shook my head. "It's not fair," I said.

"Granted," she said. "So what exactly are you going to do about it?"

I went back to Florio. "The angel says it'll work," I told him.

"Of course it'll work," he said. "I don't need any

dumb angel to tell me that."

~

It won't work, I told myself. Florio's not like that. Then I thought; well, actually he is.

All Florio ever thinks about is himself, what he wants. But what does Florio want? Stop and consider that. A man of simple tastes; raised dirt poor, so he was never handicapped like I was with expensive tastes or silly high standards, anything less than which would be a hardship. When I was a kid, anything less than the best was an affliction; we were hard done by if the bread wasn't the finest wheat maslin, baked that morning from sieved flour. When you start from such a high point, it's so much easier to be disappointed, to suffer hardship. When Florio was a boy, anything that wasn't blue with weevils living in it was grounds for joy; he experienced joy far more often than I did when he was growing up; like my grandfather in the slate quarries. Then, as he started making his way in the world, he began setting his priorities. He had no patience with anything that tended to make him weak, such as a taste for what the likes of me would regard as the good things. Weaknesses were for exploiting, not succumbing to. So he ate plain food washed down with water, never got drunk because that's when you're at your most vulnerable. Flashy clothes only serve to show people you've got money, which is blood in the water to your fellow sharks; better to look run-down and ordinary, so that the enemy underestimates you till it's too late. He quickly started making vast sums of money, but money's not for spending; if you spend it, you haven't got it anymore, and where's the sense in that? So instead of splurging on stupid status-enhancing luxuries, he ploughed back the profits of his banditry and extortion into his slum-tenement estate and especially his flourishing loan-sharking concern. The more he got, the more he lent; the more he lent, the more he got. As for other activities, forget it; he hadn't got time, for one thing, because Florio's one of those people who's never happy unless he's working, on the job, every minute of every day brings something to show for it. Women? He'd lured too many rivals to destruction with honey-traps to want anything to do with that sort of stuff. Pleasure, to Florio, was weakness. It harms you because it dilutes your concentration and you're weakened when it's taken away; you work hard to earn money, you spend it on food, booze, and loose women. What do you end up with after you've converted all that money into shit and piss and other bodily emissions? Nothing but a belly, the shakes, the clap, if you're really unlucky a bad dose of love (What was her name? Zosima? Something like that)—That would be to misunderstand entirely what money is for. Not for buying things. It's a map, to show you how far you've come. It's the only true objective way of keeping score, of knowing who's truly the better man; that and survival. To the eternal question, *How do I know if I'm doing all right?* money and still being alive provide the only valid answer, at least where Florio comes from.

So consider yourself at liberty to view him, as he views himself, as an example of that rare commodity, the free man. Others, people like me, are slaves to our upbringing, our expectations, our pleasures—No, that's wrong. I mean, it's true, but it's not the right way of putting it. Others, people like me, are hopelessly constrained because we've given away so many hostages. Do as I say, threatens Fate or the Invincible Sun, or your loved ones and your pleasures get it. Florio's invulnerable that way. The only thing you could take away from him is money, because that's all he's got, and if you do that you're his enemy, and his enemies don't tend to live long. And Florio's never had any trouble at all making money, so robbing him is really only like drawing water from a well. The level decreases for a little while, and a minute or so later it's right back where it was. Meanwhile, Florio's had you horribly killed as an example to anyone else who gets stupid ideas, and making examples like that is great for business.

An ideal candidate, therefore, for sainthood. I asked him to show me the piece of parchment again, and this time I took an intelligent interest. He'd got right to the heart of the matter, needless to say. All the land in Chosroene belongs to the king. The king lets it out to mighty nobles in return for unquestioning obedience, military service, and taxes. The nobles screw every penny they can get out of the peasants, who can't object for fear of being thrown off their land; and there are so many homeless people in Chosroene that you're never at a loss for a replacement tenant, who'll gladly agree to an extortionate rent rather than have no land at all and starve in a temple porch. Simple solution, therefore; get rid of the nobles, the whole lot of them, and let the land directly to the farmers, in small equal plots, enough to sustain life provided they work intensively. For the people who can't get farms, start factories; Chosroene exports millions of tons of food every year because nobody there can make the tools and other stuff the country needs, so they have to be bought in from Mezentia and places like that, where they make stuff instead of farming. With a little capital, you could solve all that. On the date of our arrival, the accumulated wealth in the treasury stood at one hundred million staurata (assuming an exchange rate of ten Chosroene dalers to the stauraton). It would all take time, of course—say thirty-five years, give or take—but at the end of that time, Chosroene could be converted from the armpit of Creation into the earthly paradise, and the people (who love their king) would pray for his soul till the foundations of Heaven shook—

Yes, I thought, it could work. But what about me?

~

"What about you?" the angel said.

"Yes, but—"

"Sorry if I'm being a bit slow," she went on, "but I don't see a problem. This is clearly the divine plan in action, silly of me not to have figured it out before. The Invincible Sun has heard the prayers of the suffering Chosroenes and has sent them a Redeemer. That's Florio."

"I have real problems with that."

"So what? It would take a Florio to solve the problems of Chosroene; someone brutally efficient who doesn't care who he beats up and murders, and who isn't afraid of anyone or anything; someone incorruptible, who won't be lured astray by sensual pleasure and the lusts of the flesh. A Florio would never do something like this unless his arm was twisted tight behind his back. Therefore He arranges for a Florio to be coerced into doing the job. You've got to admit, it's pretty neat."

"Yes," I said. "All fucking right. But what about me? Nobody's going to be praying for my immortal soul. I'm screwed."

"What about you?" She beamed at me. "There has to be retribution, with all this sin and wickedness going unpunished everywhere you look. That's justice; for every crime there's a criminal, everything is somebody's fault, at the end of the party someone gets stuck with the tab. Scales have to balance or everything's a mess. You were born damned. Therefore you get to carry the can. It's your function."

"That's not—"

"Yes it is." She looked at me as though I had some kind of ethical objection to two and two making four. "It's perfectly fair. You were paid for doing your job. You were born with the proverbial silver spoon firmly clamped between your jaws. Payment in advance is still payment."

I remembered something I'd said earlier. "Where's the mercy in that?"

"Mercy shmercy," said the angel. "The thing about mercy is, it's discretional. He *chooses* to forgive. If he decides not to, you can't take Him to court and get a writ of specific performance. In your case, He's decided not to. And just look at you, for crying out loud. A spoilt rich kid who thought he could get himself out of the mess he's got himself into by pulling the wings off an angel. Who could possibly ever feel the slightest sympathy for *you*?"

~

I escaped from the palace by knotting my bedsheets together and climbing out of a window. You read about people doing that and assume it's easy. It isn't. I had to let go and drop the last twelve feet. I nearly broke my leg.

Saints spend all their lives praying for an epiphany, and I'd already had one, which was more than my fair share, according to Justice. But I'd had it with Justice. So I smashed the padlock on the temple door with a brick I found in a heap of rubble, went inside and lit a lamp. By its flickering glow I was able to find the temple's most precious relic, the icon of the Double Redemption. It's a thousand years old and supposedly painted by the Redeemer himself. I took it down off the wall and held it in my left hand. In my right was the brick.

"Come down here right now," I yelled, "or the icon gets it."

I hear someone sniggering and looked round. Sitting in one of the front rows of pews was one of those crazy old women you instinctively avoid in the street. I could smell her from where I was standing. Of course, they take great care to clear people like that out of the temple before they lock up for the night.

"Go ahead," she said. "It's just an icon made with hands. And you're in so much trouble already, why not?"

I took a deep breath. Actually I wasn't scared or apprehensive at all, but I wanted to control my temper. When I get really mad I tend to stammer. "You don't give a stuff, do you?" I said. "About your hostages."

She sighed. "You don't get it," she said. "A hostage is valuable because he, she, or it is irreplaceable. For Me, there's nothing that can't be replaced. Go ahead, smash the piccy. You really do have nothing to lose."

I put the icon down on the altar. "Thank you so much for coming," I said.

"No bother," she said. "I was here anyway. I always am. I'm everywhere, all the time, but people generally don't notice."

"Whatever," I said. "I want to make a deal."

I think her nose may have twitched. "I'm listening."

"I'll free the angel," I said. "In return, I get an amnesty."

She frowned. "I can't do that. Sorry."

"Can't? You can do anything." I stopped, before I got angry and started tripping over my consonants. "Freeing a kidnapped angel is a good thing to do, right?"

She yawned. "You should've studied law," she said, "instead of theology, for which incidentally you have no aptitude whatsoever. If you'd read law, you'd know about intention."

"I know about intention just fine," I told her.

"No you don't. In criminal law, there's two parts to a crime. There's the guilty act and the guilty mind. You kill someone, that's not necessarily murder. Maybe your hand slipped or you fell out of a window onto some poor soul's head. There has to be a guilty mind as well as a guilty act."

"I know all that."

"Of course you do. Well then. Same with good deeds. There has to be a virtuous mind as well as a virtuous act.

You could free all the angels that can dance on a pinhead and you'd still get no credit for it, because your intention is saving your sorry arse. Besides," she went on, "I can't accept your offer, because that would mean breaking my promise to Florio. I did a deal, thirty-five years in exchange for the return of my angel. I can't break a promise."

"You can do anything You like."

Small smile. "I choose not to be able to break a promise," she said. "There, how's that?"

"It's not fair," I said. "What you're doing to me."

Another sigh. "Oh come on," she said. "What's justice? Observing the law. What's law? Law's the rules. Who makes the rules? I do. If only you'd been to law school, instead of wasting everybody's time at the seminary, you'd know that. In criminal law, the definition of a crime is something that's against the law. That's it, finish. They teach you that on your first day, after you've been told where to hang your coat and where the toilets are. I make the rules, the rules say you're guilty."

"Even though I've done nothing wrong?"

"Even though," she said, "you've done nothing wrong. Well, apart from not selling everything you own and giving the money to the poor. That's really bad, you know."

"Right," I said, and something clicked inside my

head. An epiphany, almost. "Fine. Suppose everybody did that, like they're supposed to? What'd happen?"

She looked at me. "Go on."

"The rich," I said, "would all be poor, and the poor would suddenly all be rich. Then what? Presumably the poor would have to sell all the stuff they bought with the money they'd got from the rich and give it to the rich, who are now the poor; and then the rich would have to give it all back. That's not the kingdom of Heaven. That's *silly*."

"There's no need to shout."

And I wasn't stammering. A miracle. "It's silly," I repeated. "The state of grace, the perfection of existence according to the rules, is a game of musical chairs. And what about the middle class? They're not poor, they're not rich either. Do they have to give to the slightly poorer and receive from the slightly richer, or do they just sit tight and handle the actual buying and selling? But then they'd be the ones who got very rich, so they'd have to give to the poor and where the hell would it ever end?" I pointed my finger at her. "You haven't thought it through, have You? It's all bullshit. Florio would never come up with a stupid scheme like that. He's doing something that makes sense. Your scheme's not a patch on his. It doesn't *work*."

She shook her head. "You're forgetting one thing," she said. "I decide what works and what doesn't. I define working. I define everything. And I make the rules."

I dropped the brick. "Then the rules are stupid," I said. "And so are you."

That annoyed her. She swelled up into a cloud of golden fire, reaching from the floor to the ceiling, infinitely reflected in all the gold leaf and gold mosaic tiles, like two mirrors facing each other. "How dare you judge Me?" she said. "Where were you when I laid the foundations of the Earth? Where were you—?"

"Oh drop dead," I said, and walked out.

~

I was halfway down the street towards the harbour when I realised I had something in my hand. I looked at it; a gold reliquary, tastelessly decorated with several ounces by weight of rubies and sapphires. I couldn't remember seeing it before, let alone stealing it. The term *fitted up* floated into my mind, Heaven knows why.

Perfect, I thought. When the Law starts planting evidence on you, at least you know you're innocent, which is a comfort. I waited till daybreak and nosed around the docks until I found a receiver of stolen goods. He gave me about one per cent of the value of the reliquary, which was plenty for my needs, and any more would've been greed, which is a sin.

One per cent was enough to pay for a berth on a ship back home to Choris, comfortable bed, wine with my dinner. Florio would probably have gone steerage to save money, but saints are like that. I went to the University, where they told me professor Saloninus was busy. I told them to tell him my name. He wasn't that busy, after all.

"What are you doing here?" he asked as I walked into his study. "You're supposed to be in Chosroene."

Living with Florio had taught me some useful skills. I got both hands round his throat before he could move. "You set me up," I said.

He made a sort of gurgling noise. I was about to kill the smartest man who ever lived, if I didn't slacken off the pressure a bit. Big deal. "You set me up," I told him. "Not God. You."

He was turning ever such a funny colour, so I eased off slightly. "I did no such thing," he wheezed.

"Yes you fucking *did*. You tricked my grandfather into committing mortal sin so he'd have to do what you told him to. Then he ducked out of eternal torment, so I'm going to have to carry the can. That was your doing, not

His. So I'm going to kill you. But not," I added, as in-spiration sputtered feebly to life inside my poor soggy brain, "in here. Outside, where He can snatch your mor-tal soul and take it down to hell, where it belongs."

I was right. That scared him. "No," he said. "Please. In here, not out there."

"You should've thought of that before you fucked me over." I forced him to his feet. "Who knows?" I said. "Maybe turning you over to Him could be my ticket out of this. Maybe that's what I have to do in order to be for-given. I could do a trade, your soul for mine. Bet you anything you like He'd rather have yours."

He tried to struggle, but Florio had taught me all about that sort of thing, bless him. I owe that man so much. "Or," I said, "because I happen to think that killing is morally wrong, you could find some other way to get me out of the shit, and then I'll let you go. But to be honest I'm more inclined to kill you. I don't think you're nearly as smart as you think you are."

I don't think Professor Saloninus was used to being shoved around; not by God, and certainly not by me. Not a great deal of difference between us, I imagine, in his eyes; two bullies. But I was that bit stronger than he was, and I had the tactical advantage. I could make him leave the room, and once we were outside it, I could kill him. I think the technical term is *force majeure*, not that it matters in the slightest.

"I know a way," he said, "if you'll just let me breathe."

"Thought you might," I said, and relaxed my grip a bit more. "The experiment, right?"

"Yes."

"You never actually said what the experiment was."

He nodded; capitulation. He wouldn't give in to physical strength, but I'd just shown a bit of intellectual muscle. "Let go of me and I'll tell you," he said. "Scouts' honour."

What else would a man swear by if he doesn't approve of God? "Fine," I said, and let him go.

In the twinkling of an eye he'd got his desk drawer open and produced a knife. I'd neglected to bring one with me. He looked at me down the blade. "Arsehole," he said. "My throat hurts like fuck."

"Serves you right. What was the experiment?"

He sat down. I could see no point in standing, so I sat down too. Suddenly it was just like a tutorial. "You're the experiment," he said. "To create a man who believes in God but sees Him for what He really is, a bully. And then," he added, "to do something about it."

"Really," I said. "Such as what?"

"He's got to go," the professor said.

Neither of us spoke for a while. "I'm sorry," I said, "I'm probably being stupid. What does go mean?"

"Die," said the professor. "He's got to die. We've got to kill Him."

Oh dear. The smartest man in the world, completely out of his gourd. And now he had a knife, so hauling him outside and strangling him would be that much harder. My own stupid fault, for trying to be merciful.

"I know," he was saying, "it's a drastic step, I admit that. For one thing, who's to say that once He's gone, things will be any better? They could be a whole lot worse. Just because His regime is indescribably shitty, it doesn't follow that there's a better way. It's like what the Vesani say about democracy, it's a ghastly, terrible system but it's better than the alternatives. Trouble is, we have no choice, not anymore. We've committed ourselves. Unless we want to burn in hell, there's no other course open to us."

Welcome to the end of my rope. "Stop talking like that," I pleaded, "it makes my head hurt. You can't kill God. You just *can't*. It's not possible."

I'd disappointed him. "Just when I thought you were starting to show promise," he said. "Didn't you ever listen to anything in my lectures?"

Now I just felt tired; completely exhausted. "I think I may have missed that bit."

"God," said the professor, "can do anything. Right?"

"I suppose so, yes. Except," I pointed out, "in here."

"Forget about in here. God can do anything."

"Yes."

"So He can die."

"Yes, but—" I stopped. Anything? "Yes."

"Very good. He can die. So we kill him."

Too tired to argue. "And how would you propose going about that?"

"Wrong question," said the professor. "What you should've asked was, what can God die of? To which the answer is—?"

"Pass," I said.

"Despair."

For crying out loud. "Despair," I repeated. "Fine. That's really helpful."

"Despair," said the professor, "because nobody believes in Him anymore. Because His entire creation has turned their back on Him, and everything He's done has turned out to be worthless, nothing. He couldn't handle that. So He'd die."

I'd sort of lost interest. "If you say so, professor."

"I say so. Trust me, I'm the smartest man in the

world. All I have to do is demonstrate that He doesn't exist, and—"

"But He does."

Saloninus rolled his eyes. "Yes, but only you and I and Florio *know* that. Everybody else just believes. Besides, once I've proved it, it'll be true."

"No it won't."

"Yes it will, because He'll die. And then it *will* be true. That's how the truth is formed. Or hadn't you grasped that?"

And then, just as I was about to give the whole thing up as a bad job and try and kill Saloninus out of pure disgust and probably get myself stabbed in the process—You might well call it an epiphany. Certainly it was the Word of God that inspired me. "Professor," I said. "What's gravity?"

He frowned. "Never heard of it."

"Me neither. But He told me about it, or at least He mentioned it. He said something about a magnification-to-gravity ratio, which turned out to be a dumb joke about the bigger they are, the harder they fall. Magnification I can understand, it's making things bigger. But what's gravity?"

"Search me," said the professor. "Unless—"

That's not how it's usually told, of course. In the usual

story, Saloninus is sitting under an apple tree in his garden, and an apple falls on his head, and suddenly he understands. Gravity! A force that makes things fall; but ever so much more than that. It's a ray of light shining out from the crack under a closed door. He opens the door, and sees the sun. Not the Invincible Sun, that man-made fable, but the real thing. Suddenly he knows how the world really works. Not God. A machine.

"It's going to take me awhile," he said. "To figure out the implications of all this."

"You might want to get a wiggle on," I said. "You've got slightly less than thirty-five years."

He smiled at me. "Leave it with me," he said.

~

That was thirty years ago. Trust the smartest man in the world to deliver, under budget and ahead of schedule.

I'd be the last one to say that the new regime is better than the old one. Actually, it's a whole lot worse. Take, for example, Chosroene. Florio easily persuaded the population to go along with his ideas because he told them he was doing God's will. In just under four years, he'd confiscated the vast estates controlled by the nobles and distributed the land among the peasants. A year after that, all the small manufacturers he'd financed out of the royal treasury were up and running and starting to show a profit. Nobody was starving, nobody was out of work, everybody was better off except for the old aristocracy (inherited wealth; enough said). Twenty years of growing prosperity and social justice; and then Saloninus' epoch-making book, *Principia Mathematica*, turned everything on its head. Within six months it was being read and understood as far afield as Chosroene, where there were riots and blood flowed in rivers in the gutters as the howling mobs eviscerated the old priesthood, furious at having been duped for so long. In the general chaos that followed, the surviving aristocrats promised to restore order, which they did, quickly and efficiently, along with a complete return to the old ways. Florio managed to escape by knotting sheets together and climbing out of his window (I could have told him it's not as easy as it sounds; he twisted his ankle and walks with a limp to this day) but everything he'd achieved was swept away without leaving a trace behind. He came back to Choris and resumed his previous calling. One of the first things he did, in fact, was drop in on me in the middle of the night and remind me that I still owed him a quarter of a million staurata.

Fortunately I was able to pay him back, with interest, without even having to go to the bank. When Saloninus approached Periboeus the bookseller with the manuscript of *Principia*, Periboeus wasn't interested; a great read, he said, very thought-provoking but with limited appeal; not for us, he didn't think. But Saloninus offered him a new sort of deal. Periboeus wouldn't have to pay him anything for it, not right away. Instead, for every copy he sold, he'd give Saloninus thirty trachy, out of a cover price of a half stauraton. Periboeus couldn't resist a deal like that. Sometime afterwards, Saloninus told me I could have twenty trachy out of every stauraton he made from the book, as a gesture of goodwill, to cover any inconvenience I'd been put to in the course of the experiment. It was, he said, the very least he could do. I agreed with him. It was.

God died about eighteen months ago of, so they say, a broken heart. His last public appearance was to the high priest of the Golden Spire in Urbissima, but He did pay one more visit before He lay down and died. He came to see me.

"I'll get you for this," He said.

"No," I told Him, "you won't. I've still got five years

left to run, and you're bound by your promise. By that time, you'll be history. Well, theology. Face it," I added, "you lost. We won."

He glared at me. "I can do anything," He said. "I can flatten you with a thunderbolt right now. There'd be nothing left except glass and a nasty smell."

He wasn't looking well. Thin, drawn, pale, bags under His eyes. He reminded me of my mother, just before the end, when she stopped eating because she couldn't keep anything down; and that reminded me of why He had to go. "No," I said, "you couldn't. You made a promise. Thirty-five years."

"I can break my promises. I can do anything."

I felt a certain amount of pity, but mostly contempt. "Not," I said, "for much longer."

And that was my final epiphany. Not long after that there was a total eclipse that lasted for forty-eight hours; a week after that there was the most appalling smell, which went on for considerably longer. Now there's nothing at all.

I did that. Well, Saloninus and I did it together. I guess I can honestly say I know the nature and quality of my actions. I can also say I'm truly sorry for them. I asked Florio what happened to the angel. He said he has no idea. Presumably she's still there, in her cage;

because it isolated her from Him, I imagine it also protected her from His death. Since she was a part of Him, that would mean that a part of Him still survives, isolated, protected, completely cut off by the genius of Saloninus, the smartest man who ever lived. In which case maybe someday—

That's how I console myself, when I look around at the general misery I see everywhere, now that He's gone, caused by His going. After all, I tell myself, He could do anything. Which meant that He could die; which also means that He can rise again from the dead, should He choose to do so, should we ever feel the need to release Him from the cage. In fact I might just do that, some day, when the despair gets too much for me to bear. Until then, He palpably doesn't exist and so I don't believe in Him, as I stated earlier in this narrative. Which makes everything my own bloody stupid fault, nobody else's, not my grandfather's, not the professor's, not God's; mine. Serves me right. No matter what you do or don't believe, pulling the wings off angels is a profoundly horrible, stupid thing to do, and in the long run you'll find you wish you hadn't.

The professor sees things differently. All his life, he told me, he'd been poor as a rat; the smartest man in the history of the world, with nothing but his professor's salary and a few extra trachy here and there, mostly gained by illegitimate means. Now he's so rich he'll never have to work again; no more teaching pig-ignorant students, no more writing epoch-making books that change the fundamental nature of human existence. As far as he's concerned, the death of God is the best thing that's ever happened to him.

Well. It's a point of view.

# About the Author

Having worked in journalism, numismatics, and the law, **K. J. PARKER** now writes for a precarious living. He is the author of *Devices and Desires, Evil for Evil, The Devil You Know*, and other novels. K. J. Parker also writes under the name Tom Holt and has won the World Fantasy Award twice.

# TOR·COM

**Science fiction. Fantasy. The universe.**

**And related subjects.**

\*

More than just a publisher's website, *Tor.com*
is a venue for **original fiction, comics,** and
**discussion** of the entire field of SF and fantasy,
in all media and from all sources. Visit our site
today—and join the conversation yourself.